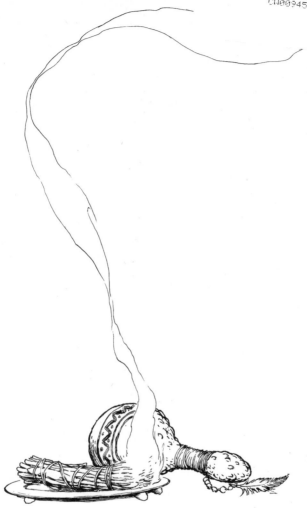

Medicine Road

Tachyon Publications

Charles de LinT

Medicine Road

Illustrated by Charles Vess

Cover art and illustrations
copyright © 2004 by Charles Vess
Interior design by John Coulthart
Cover design by Ann Monn

Tachyon Publications
1459 18th Street #139
San Francisco, CA 94107
(415) 285-5615
www.tachyonpublications.com
tachyon@tachyonpublications.com

Series Editor: Jacob Weisman

ISBN 13: 978-1-892391-88-9
ISBN 10: 1-892391-88-0

Printed in the United States
of America by Worzalla

First Tachyon Publications
edition: 2009

9 8 7 6 5 4 3 2

Acknowledgments

Special thanks to Terri Windling for introducing me to the Hole, not to mention the Sonoran Desert; to Kim Antieau for sharing snake stories; Mardelle Kunz for Tucson fact-checking; Julie Bartel Thomas for doing her librarian bit and tracking down some needed info on short notice; Karen Shaffer for canyon fact-checking; Charles Vess for some wonderfully inspiring sketches that he did at the beginning of this project; Bill Schafer for making it all possible; and MaryAnn (there's no one else with whom I'd rather share the spirit of the desert) for her editing and continued support.

Musical thanks go out to Calexico (wish I'd been at that show in Roskilde), the late Joe Strummer (for all his great music, but especially — for this book — for the soundtrack to *Walker*), Barbara Luna, Los Lobos, Luz Casal, Los de Abajo, Mecano (for "Una Rosa es una Rosa"), Ottmar Leibert, Shakira (the Spanish-language material), Ojos de Brujo, Urubamba, Los Ninos de Sara (for "Mi...Angel"), Robbie Robertson, Marty Stuart (especially for the *All the Pretty Horses* soundtrack), Bill Frisell (for his Americana excursions), Ian Tamblyn, Douglas Spotted Eagle, and Peter Kater.

We actually took the same road trip that Laurel and Bess do in these pages. By "we," I mean some of the folks already mentioned above: MaryAnn, the other Charles (LC), Karen, Terri, Julie, and Mardelle. Also in the posse were Kenny Bartel, Anna Young, and Richard Kunz. Mardelle and Richard, unfortunately, only came as far as Prescott — now they get to see what they missed, because we had a grand time, indeed.

And speaking of grand times, if you get half as much enjoyment out of reading this book as I did writing it, I'll be well pleased.

CHARLES DE LINT
OTTAWA, WINTER 2003

Contents

dedicated to
the memory of my father-in-law
John Roy Harris

he always did enjoy
a good road trip

CdL

Red Dog chasing, Jackalope
out in the badlands, that's the way it can go
driven by hunger, looking for something
deep in the desert, deep in the soul

medicine wheel, dreams in the moonlight
from each direction, the four winds blow
Coyote Woman, she has a vision
sets them to travel, on the Medicine Road

they're on the Medicine Road, out in the desert
thunder is talking, rumbling low
bound by a promise, laid upon them
to help each other, on the Medicine Road

in the flight of the hawk, there is a mystery
in the sound of a flute, hear a raven's cry
in the beat of a drum, there is a heartbeat
in the eyes of a lover, is a medicine sky

smoke is rising, sage and sweetgrass
smoke is rising, like an eagle's flight
smoke is rising, tobacco burning
smoke is rising, from a medicine pipe

brothers and sisters, are guided by spirits
some follow the Ghost Dance, some the buffalo
los peyoteros, are guided by Mescal
Coyote's children, take the Medicine Road

they're on the Medicine Road, out in the desert
thunder is talking, rumbling low
bound by a promise, laid upon them
to help each other, on the Medicine Road

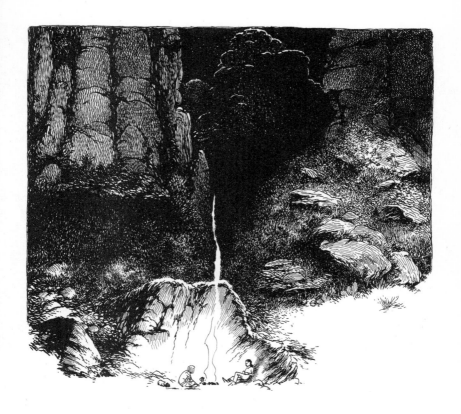

Changing Dog and Corn Hair

ONE NIGHT, NOT so long ago, Changing Dog and Corn Hair met up in Sedona, Arizona, to have a talk about an old bargain they'd made with Coyote Woman. It's funny, thinking of the two of them together like that; I can imagine them doing pretty much anything except getting along. Most times they'll argue the color of the moon, or the taste of water, if they can't find something better to disagree on. There's nothing much they ever seem to settle on, except that the other's wrong.

But this night, Corn Hair wasn't aiming for an argument. She had herself a camp there by Oak Creek, on the south bank where the water runs below Cathedral Rock. It wasn't much, just her bedroll laid out in the sand under the sycamores, with her pack doubling as a pillow. Close by, she'd built a small fire on which she was boiling water in a tin coffeepot, the bottom blackened from all its years of use. She ground some coffee beans using a flat rock and another the size of her fist for a mortar and pestle, scooping them into the now-boiling water when they were ground to her satisfaction. By the time Changing Dog came ambling down from the red rock scars skirting the solitary butte that towered above the creek, the coffee was thick and black, ready to drink.

Changing Dog nodded hello and sat cross-legged near the fire. He was a rangy, copper-skinned man with a narrow face and long, chestnut hair that streaked to a dark tan at his temples and was kept tied back with a thin strip of leather. You hardly ever saw him dressing up. That night he was wearing a white T-shirt and jeans, dusty tooled-leather cowboy boots and an old brown leather jacket going thin at the elbows. He wasn't a homely man and he wasn't particularly handsome, but he had these eyes that would grab anybody's attention, especially a woman's. They were a vivid cornflower blue that looked violet in the right light, and there was always a promise in them — not that he'd necessarily deliver, but that whatever might come, it would at least be interesting.

He accepted the tin coffee mug that Corn Hair handed him and took an appreciative sip. Setting the mug in the sand, he pulled a tobacco pouch from his pocket and rolled them each a cigarette, lighting them with a twig from the fire. He left one hanging from his lips, offering the other to Corn Hair.

"So one of the crows found you," she said as she took the cigarette.

Changing Dog nodded. "I was surprised to get the message."

"Are you telling me you've lost track of the days?"

"Oh, I know what day it is coming up. I've been counting them off for a hundred years, same as you."

Corn Hair had a couple of puffs from the cigarette he'd given her, just to be polite, then dropped the butt into the fire. She wasn't a smoker herself and that was about the only easy definition you could apply to her. Never wholly a part of this world before the night the two of them met Coyote Woman, she still wasn't much a part of it now either, though at least she looked closer to belonging.

She was maybe a head shorter than Changing Dog, which made her closer to five-two than five-three, and she dressed for comfort in the high desert country: thick cotton khaki cargo pants, tan jersey, fringed-leather vest with beadwork below either shoulder, and a pair of good leather walking shoes. Her jacket hung from a nearby tree at the moment, a three-quarter length wool coat that, with all its colored patterns, might have been made from a Navajo blanket.

In the firelight her shoulder-length hair looked blonde, but in the sun you noticed all the different streaks from dark corn yellow to almost white. She wasn't skinny, but she wasn't close to overweight. Her features always reminded me of a hare or a deer: long, but still slightly rounded, with a pair of sleepy brown eyes that mesmerize you. Her skin held a pattern like the bark of the sycamores, ranging from dark brown patches to those almost white — it was her only real holdover after the change, carrying the pattern of her fur on her skin when she became a woman.

"So what are you saying?" she asked. "Have you gone and got yourself tired of these five-fingered shapes we're using?"

Changing Dog took a long drag and blew it out. "And lose having the best of two worlds? Not likely."

"I don't see you doing much to help."

"True love's not like you looking for a certain rock in the desert, or chasing down just the right word you need for one of those songs of yours."

Corn Hair nodded. "Don't you think I know that? But at least I've got someone."

"And you made that happen?"

"No, but at least I was available. At least I was meeting people. If you screw this up —"

"I know. I screw it up for both of us." Changing Dog regarded her from across the fire, that promise in his eyes working their magic. "I still say we should be together."

Corn Hair didn't bother to protest. She just smiled and said, "Like that's ever going to happen."

中 中 中

I think you need to know how the lives of these two got so tangled up in each other's in the first place.

A hundred years ago, Sedona was a different place. Oh, the red rock mesas were here, just like they are now, the ponderosa pines climbing up their sides. Oak and sycamores followed the path of the creek. But back then, it didn't even have a name. That didn't come until T. C. Schnebly, the first postmaster, got the area a postal station in the early part of the twentieth century and named it after his wife.

Indians lived here pretty much as long as anyone can remember — unless you're Coyote Woman, but she's been around for so long she remembers things no one else can. They settled near Oak Creek, raising corn, beans, and squash. The Europeans didn't start showing up until the 1870s, and by 1902, the year a red dog chased a jackalope up to the Cathedral Rock vortex, there were only twenty families living in the area.

Cathedral Rock didn't have a name then either, nor did the vortex, and the New Agers weren't even born. If you mentioned the word *vortex* to anyone living along Oak Creek in those days, all you'd get back was a blank look. The sacred places didn't have names, just like the tribes of the first people, the animal people who were here before even the Indians, didn't have names. Everybody knew who everybody else was. You asked after Rattlesnake and people knew which one you meant, but I can't explain how. The tribes had a different way of hearing things, I guess.

Coyote Woman was around then, just like she's always been and probably always will. She's not bound by the past or the future. She just lives in the now, but that now's always happening, so you meet her in your now and there's no telling what now she's in. I guess that's even more confusing. Maybe this is easier: think of time as a spiral instead of a straight line. The past and the future are on the spiral, twisting this way, curving that way, now's in the center of it all. Step out of the now and you can move in any direction you want.

Kind of like the Cathedral Rock vortex, I suppose, except it's always turning in a sunwise direction — what we'd call clockwise now.

So Coyote Woman's there, doing whatever she does in a place like that — talking to the medicine man who lives inside the rock at the base of the spires, maybe — and who comes running in to disturb her but this red dog with the look of a coyote about him, chasing a jackalope. I don't need to tell you what a jackalope is, do I? They're part jackrabbit, part deer — kind of like the best of both, the way a mule is compared to the horse and donkey that give him his genes; and like the mule, they can't breed. But they're stronger than either of the tribes that joined to put them in this world. Not just physically, but inside, in the heart and spirit, too.

Now Coyote Woman's a lot like her brother Cody — always getting this itch to fix a thing even when it's none of her business — but being a woman, she doesn't always make such a mess of it. When she sees this pair — doing what comes natural, after all, because a dog's got to eat and a jackalope doesn't want to be anybody's meal — she gets it in her head to give them something else to think about.

There was a time when all the tribes could wear whichever shape they wanted, animal or human, and there's still some walking this world who can. But most of us have forgotten, and this dog and jackalope, they each came from a long line of forgetters. So what Coyote Woman does is she gives that gift back to them, but she puts a price on it, because everything costs something, even back then. There's never been a free ride, just a different coin.

She tells them they can keep this gift forever, but to do that she only allows them a hundred years to find themselves a soul mate — someone who loves them unconditionally for who they really are. The catch is, they both have to find that true love before the hundred years are up, or neither gets to keep the gift. She figures looking for that will keep them from bothering each other for some time. Maybe even teach them to help each other.

"When those hundred years are up," she says, "I'll come see you both out at the Medicine Wheel, find out how you've done."

Well, a hundred years is a long time to anybody who only had a natural life span to look forward to before they got a gift like that. Those two looked at each other, two five-fingered beings standing there naked in the moonlight, then they each walked away, one went one way, the other took the opposite direction, and it was a long time before they saw each other again.

But the trouble is, a hundred years can also go by pretty damn quick, you're not paying attention to it. All too soon these two realized that time was running out. Corn Hair, she gave up some of her solitary ways — which involved a lot of time in the desert, studying on the heart and soul of ceremonies and spirits — and made the effort to interact with others more. It wasn't easy to find a soul mate, not like Coyote Woman wanted, because Corn Hair had her own terms to be met before she'd let somebody else into her life like that. But she found him, a painter, as full of love for the desert as she was, always ready to be with her, but given to his own solitary ways as well, seeing how he was a painter.

But Changing Dog was a different story. Unlike Corn Hair, he was a social dog, but he couldn't commit. Didn't want to, the truth be told, and women, they'd see that. They'd have fun with him, they'd be friends and lovers and a few of them even took him on as a special project, see if they couldn't change his rambling ways, but it never took. As the years and months and finally the weeks grew closer to the night when Coyote Woman would be coming to take their measure, Corn Hair realized that her own gift was about to be lost.

That's why she asked the crows to give a message to Changing Dog, why they were talking now.

"I can't be anybody else but who I am," Changing Dog told her.

He was rolling another cigarette, but this time Corn Hair shook her head when he offered it to her. Changing Dog shrugged and got it lit. There was a look in his eyes as he blew out a stream of blue-grey smoke that told Corn Hair he was genuinely sorry, but sorry didn't help. She sighed.

"You should have been called Can't Change Dog," she said. "Maybe even Won't Change Dog."

"I'm Changing Dog because I'm never one thing for long."

"Have you never really cared for one other person?" she asked, because it didn't matter to Coyote Woman if your true love was male and female. The love just had to be true.

"Besides you?"

"I'm being serious."

"Maybe I am, too."

And there was that promise in his eyes, but Corn Hair could never tell if it was a promise to be true, or a promise to break her heart. It didn't matter either way. She already had her true love.

She sighed again. The moon was just a sliver of its first quarter, rising above the red rock mesas in the eastern sky. She watched the smoke from Changing Dog's cigarette meet the smoke from her fire, the two of them spiraling in a braid up into the dark sky, losing themselves there among the stars the way the present can get lost when the past and the future come sniffing around, and all you're trying to do is make it through the day that's in front of you.

Come the next dark of the moon, Coyote Woman would be calling in her markers.

"We've got less than a month to live," she said.

Changing Dog shook his head. "She's not going to kill us. She's just going to change us back into what we were."

Corn Hair thought about the life she'd made for herself, half in this world, half in the animal. She thought of her painter with his strong hands and deep love, of his kind eyes and the way he could make her shiver without even having to touch her.

She gave Changing Dog a sad look that he obviously didn't understand. "What?" he asked. "Why are you looking at me like that?"

"Maybe for me, losing the gift and dying are pretty much the same thing."

"Don't talk crazy."

If that was talking crazy, then Corn Hair decided not to talk at all. She sat there, stoic and silent, refusing to reply to a single thing Changing Dog had to say until he finally got up and walked away, back into the night.

She stayed like that for a long while, until the moon sliver was almost directly overhead. Then finally she stirred. She took a sage smudge stick and a small painted gourd rattle out of her pack. Lighting the smudge stick, she used its smoke to bless the four directions. Then she put it out and laid it on the sand. She picked up the rattle and woke a simple rhythm.

"Hey-ya hey-ya hey-ya," she sang, her singing voice higher and not as husky as her speaking voice. "Ya-ha-hey. Hey-ya hey-ya hey-ya."

She sang to the spirits, calling a blessing on them and the land and her painter. She didn't ask them for help. Help was something the spirits would give or not by their own whim. Mostly they expected people to help each other. To help themselves.

"Hey-ya hey-ya hey-ya."

One Night in the Hole

Bess Dillard

"WHY DOES EVERYONE think I'm gay?" Laurel asked.

I gave my sister a look. "There's nothing wrong with being gay."

"I didn't say there was. I just want to know why people think *I* am."

"People like who?"

"Like that woman at the table by the door who's been staring at me all night like she wants to take all my clothes off — you know, the way a guy looks at you."

I stole a surreptitious look at the attractive dark-haired native woman that Laurel had to be talking about. She was dressed all in black — jeans, boots, T-shirt, bolero jacket, with a flat-brimmed black hat sitting on the bar beside her beer — and was wearing an incredible amount of turquoise jewelry: earrings, a half-dozen bracelets on either arm, rings on almost every finger, necklaces and a choker, more still sewn into her jacket and on her hatband. But for some reason, instead of appearing showy or affected, it worked.

"Maybe it's just that she's gay," I said.

Laurel harrumphed.

"Or maybe she just really likes excellent fiddle-playing."

"Now you're sucking up."

I smiled. "You should go talk to her. Sell her a CD."

We'd just finished playing our first set at the Hole, in Tucson, Arizona, and were getting ready to take our break. The place was properly called the Hole in the Wall, but when we asked directions to the Barrio Historica at the front desk of our hotel, the guy with the purple hair told us everyone just calls it the Hole. He also told us that it's pretty much a dive, but he should see the roadhouses back home in the Kickaha Mountains. This old adobe building, right on the edge of the barrio, is like a palace compared to some of the places we've played in Tyson County.

And it's très cool, as Frenchy'd say.

You come in off the street into a warren of rooms with saguaro rib ceilings, thick adobe walls, beautifully carved oak doors, and weathered wood plank floors. It smells of mesquite and beer, cigarette smoke and salsa. The band posters on the walls advertise everything from Tex-Mex and Cajun to bluegrass, reggae, and plain old rock 'n' roll.

But the best part is that once you've threaded your way through the maze of little inner rooms, you come out into a central courtyard, open to the sky. Clematis vines crawl up the walls. Mismatched tables are scattered across a cracked tile floor. And there, under the spreading branches of a mesquite tree, is the stage where we've been playing.

It's a far cry from Tyson County, all right. But everything's been different for us since we took our music on the road.

Back home there's more of us red-haired Dillard girls than you can shake a stick at — seven of us sisters; nine girls altogether if you include our mother and Adie's little baby Lily. We range from the hopefully urbane, like me and Laurel, to our hillbilly sister Sarah Jane, who lives alone up on a mountaintop in the hills in back of the farm where Mama and our other sisters live. I guess Laurel and I've still got some twang in our voices, but we've been touring for a couple of years now, meeting all kinds of people, all over the country, and talking with them has rubbed some of the raw edges off the way we talk.

Least I hope it has. It's not that I'm ashamed of our roots or anything. It's just that the twang makes people think we're dumb hicks and that gets old pretty fast. Especially when it's some club owner trying to cheat us out of what we're owed for a gig, or some slick city boy trying to talk us into bed. I can't tell you how many times we've heard, "So you're twins. Do you like to do *everything* together?" followed by a leer and a wink.

But they're the exceptions. Most folks that come to see us play, or happen on a gig in a bar like this and stay because they like the music, are good folks. The kind that don't set any warning bells ringing in our heads.

When we finish a set we've taken to sitting and chatting with people in the audience — and not to sell CDs. We figure, if folks like our music, we've probably got something in common with them, and when you're far from home, this is pretty much the best way for us to meet like-minded folks. It also raises the odds of getting picked up — which isn't necessarily a bad thing — but it's not something we actively pursue on a regular basis. Doesn't stop us from talking about it, though.

"Well, I like the red-haired guy at the corner table," I told my sister.

"His hair's not red," she said. "Our hair is red. His is more chestnut."

"Whatever. He's been looking at me all night and I'd like to see what he's all about."

"Why don't you go sell *him* a CD?"

I picked up my beer and stood. "Maybe I just will."

"Aw, don't leave me on my own," Laurel said. "The next thing you know that woman's going to be hitting on me and then where am I going to be?"

"Flattered?"

"You wish."

"Maybe she'll give you a piece of that turquoise jewelry — she's sure got enough of it."

"Bess..."

"I'd hold out for one of those bracelets," I said, then I stepped off the stage and made my way to the corner table.

Thomas Young

The moon had risen outside Thomas's studio, its silvery light illuminating the painting that he had placed on his easel. When the wind picked up for a moment, the distinctive smell from the creosote bushes followed the moonlight in through the window, strong over the faint scent of turps and spirits that normally hung in the studio air.

Thomas loved that smell — had from the first time he'd moved here from back east, which was why he'd planted the bushes around the studio. Their scent was strongest after a rain, but never entirely absent.

He loved the moonlight, too. It gave the commonest view a sense of cool mystery.

Alice called it spirit light. It was born, she said, in the gaze of *los santos* and the spirits of the desert. Saguaro and hawk. Mouse and snake and lizard. A quick light, but slow, too. The way a dream moves quick and slow at the same time. The way time does, depending on if you're anticipating something or need more of it.

Thomas sighed. He sat in the shadows, thinking of light, listening to the distant *yip-yip-yip* of coyotes, his gaze on the painting.

It was an old piece, one he'd never put in a show, one he wouldn't even consider selling. A young Alice looked back at him from that canvas — an Alice with drooping jackrabbit ears and small antlers lifting from her blonde hair, the way he saw her in his mind's eye ever since she'd told him of her curious origin. The scene behind her had been painted in the foothills of the Rincons, which started their climb from the desert floor only a few miles from the studio.

A young Alice.

Thinking that brought a bittersweet smile to Thomas's lips.

"I can't say what will happen with us," she'd told him thirty years ago when they first decided to live together. "But I won't be the one to leave. Not so long as you love me."

He'd been a young, unknown painter in those days. A year into his thirties and just beginning to make his mark on the burgeoning scene of the Southwestern art movement. He was sixty-two now and never had to worry about finding a gallery to hang his work. They came to him now, from as far away as New York and Europe and Japan.

Much had changed for him, but Alice...Alice was unchanged. She looked the same, while his hair greyed and thinned and the roadmap of wrinkles grew upon his face as quickly as the city of Tucson spread out into the desert.

And he still loved her. But he wasn't sure she loved him anymore.

She didn't look at him any differently. That great warmth still flowed into him when she smiled at him, or laid a hand on his arm, or leaned against him. But more and more he got the sense that she was saying good-bye. To the house. To her beloved garden.

To him.

And he didn't know why.

He had the feeling that one day soon she would disappear back into the desert as mysteriously as she'd come out of it that day they'd first met.

He kept wanting to talk to her about it, but he'd never been good with words. Still wasn't. He couldn't begin to figure out which to use for what he really needed to know.

Was she really leaving him?

When was she leaving him?

Why was she leaving him?

He knew he needed to talk to her, before it was too late. He knew he should get up right now and go to the bedroom where she was probably still reading. If he still didn't have the words, he could just hold her.

But all he could do was sit here in the studio, staring at the painting.

Already missing her.

Outside in the desert, the coyotes cried again, a lonesome, distant sound that expressed so perfectly the lonesome, distant feeling that had taken up an unwanted residence in his heart.

Jim Changing Dog

I've been watching her all night, but it looks like I wasn't being close to subtle, because now she's making a beeline straight for my table. And I can't read her mood at all. Is she coming over because she's interested, or is she going to tell me off?

But the thing is, I just couldn't take my eyes off her from the moment I walked into the Hole. I never even looked around to see who else is here tonight, though they've got a pretty good crowd for an unknown bluegrass duo — at least one that I never heard of. Probably helps that they're twins, young and pretty, and damned talented, if the set I've just heard is any indication. But while she and her sister are identical, their energy isn't, and this one making her way to where I'm sitting is starting to wake something deep in my chest, not to mention causing a different kind of stirring in my jeans. Good thing these tables don't have glass tops.

She looks down at me when she gets to where I'm sitting, standing over me with one hand on her hip, red hair held back with an elastic hair tie that's having a hard time taming her mass of long curls. This close I see that those luminous eyes of hers are more blue than grey. I like the spray of freckles under them. They're like a familiar constellation, friendly and warm under the cool mystery of her eyes.

"So how come you've been staring at me all night?" she asks, bold as brass.

"You're on stage, aren't you? I'd think you'd want people paying attention to you."

I smile to take any possible sting out of my words.

"You know what I mean," she says.

I relent and give her a nod. "I've been waiting to meet you for a long time."

That makes her relax, though I'm guessing we're taking different meanings from those words. I figure she's thinking I'm a fan of the band, happy to finally see them live. But the truth is, while I have been looking for her, I didn't know it was her in particular until I walked into the Hole tonight.

"Can I get you a drink?" I ask.

She holds up a half-full bottle of Negra Modelo and shakes her head. "I'm good."

I don't know what to do with my hands — wouldn't that make Alice smile, to see me worried about making a good impression. But this could be important. This *is* important.

I busy my fingers by rolling a cigarette and then offer it to her. She shakes her head again. Shakes it a third time when I ask her whether she minds if I indulge.

"Is this your first time seeing us?" she asks.

I nod. "I've never even heard of you before tonight, but I love what I'm hearing."

She gives me a puzzled look. "But you said you've been waiting a long time to see us."

"I did."

"But...did you hear about the gig from our Internet mailing list?"

I shake my head. "I don't have an address."

"You're not online?" she asks, like I just grew an extra head.

"I mean I don't even have a postal address."

Now she looks really puzzled.

"I just knew *you* were out there somewhere," I say.

The puzzled look goes all the way to wary, like she hasn't heard variations on this a thousand times before, and her body language says she'd maybe like more than a table between us.

Slow down, I tell myself. You're coming on too strong.

"Don't worry," I say aloud. "I'm not stalking you."

"Like you'd admit if you were."

"I guess that's true."

"So what did you mean?"

I shrug and take a last drag from my cigarette, butting it out in the ashtray. We both follow the action with our gazes. When I look up from the smoldering butt, our gazes meet. I don't look away.

"It's just the way you play your instruments," I say. "The way you sing those old songs. I know this is just another gig for you, and I'm just some guy sitting here in the audience, but the music makes me feel connected to something bigger and older than either one of us. I guess what I'm trying to say is, I've been waiting for something like that for a long time. I just didn't know I was until it happened to me tonight."

There's the whisper of a smile in the corner of her mouth and her eyes warm up a little, but there's still that hint of wariness sitting in the back of them. I figure she's going to say some make-nice thing that musicians say when they want to extract themselves from a situation like this, but she surprises me.

"Do you believe in fairy tales?" she asks.

I don't even hesitate.

"Yes," I tell her.

"No, I mean do you *really* believe they're real."

"Yes."

She looks at me, trying to see what I'm really thinking. I keep my eyes guileless and return her gaze.

"You were supposed to fail that test," she says.

"Why?"

"I don't know. Just everybody does."

"And would you prefer that I had?"

She gives her head a slow shake. The wariness is almost completely gone.

"Your eyes are actually violet," she says.

"So I've been told. Not much I can do about it."

"You say that like having beautiful eyes is a bad thing."

Now she's almost flirting with me, but I pretend to pay it no mind.

"I like to look on a pretty girl as much as the next guy," I tell her, "and I don't mind someone thinking maybe I don't look too bad, but that's all just surface, you know? It's in our genes — something we don't have any real control over. What's more important is when someone tells you that you've got a good heart. That they trust you. That they know they can count on you."

"And can people?"

I smile. "I'm a bad liar."

"What gives you away?"

She's definitely flirting.

"Nothing does," I say. "I just can't put my heart into it. I find it easier to say what I mean and keep my promises."

"Promises," she repeats and I know she's seeing them in my eyes, the way Alice says women always do.

If I knew how to turn it down, I would, but all I can do is change the subject, slow things down a little by putting our attention on something else.

"Are you in town for very long?" I ask her.

She blinks, like she has to clear her mind and shift gears, then shrugs. "Just a couple more days. We've got a house concert in Sedona and before that a bar gig in a place called Jerome —"

"You'll love it there. It's built right into the side of the mountain."

She nods. "Yeah, I looked it up on the Internet. It does look kind of cool. Before those we're playing another house concert in, um, Prescott. That's this coming Saturday night."

I correct her pronunciation. "Say, 'Presc'tt.' Otherwise, people will really know you're not a local."

"But I'm not, so what does it matter?"

"I suppose that's true. And after Sedona?"

"We're back here, opening for Darlene Flatt & the Piney Wood Ramblers at the Rialto on the following Friday night. Darlene's from up around the same part of Tyson County as we come from, and we've played a bunch with the Ramblers back home, but it was still pretty cool of them to ask us to do this gig."

"Friends in high places."

She smiles. "Something like that. Or a least a little higher up the ladder than we are."

"So how are you getting around?"

"I'm not sure right now. I guess we'll have to rent a car. We thought we'd bus it, but I went to the Greyhound Web site before we left Newford and it doesn't look like they have service to Jerome or Sedona, although they do go to Prescott." She gives me a grin as she emphasizes her mispronunciation. "It'll eat into our savings, but at least we'll get to see a bit of the countryside."

"I could drive you."

"Yeah, right."

The wariness is back in her eyes — no more than a faint flutter, but it's there.

"No, seriously. I'm between jobs at the moment and I'd love to hear more of your music."

"I don't know..."

What she really means is, I don't know *you*.

"I won't lie," I tell her. "You're pretty as all get-out and if this hadn't come up, I'd have had to try to think of some other way to get to see more of you."

"What happened to your telling me that it's what's inside that matters?"

"That hasn't changed. But I can't know what's inside unless I get to know you better, and I'd like to do that on both counts. But the bottom line is, you tell me to walk and I'll get up out of this chair and head for the exit."

"You're kind of forward, aren't you?"

"Hey, I didn't come walking up to your table."

She gives me a grin. "That's true. And you even paid to get in — you did pay to get in, right?"

"Of course I did. At least tonight."

"Maybe I'm just trying to sell you a CD."

"Well, you're doing a good job of it," I say, "because I'm ready to buy one."

She laughs and shakes her head. I feel something lift inside my chest. Damn, but she's pretty. I wasn't lying about wanting to connect to what she's got inside. But damn, she's pretty.

"Well, think about it," I say. "The trip. There'll be no strings attached and I'll find my own accommodations. I'll just be your driver."

"That's asking a lot of you."

"It's just friendly, Southwestern hospitality. But I do expect to get into the gigs for free. And if I get your company on the drive between towns, well, it sounds like a good deal to me."

She thinks about it for a moment.

"I'll have to ask my sister," she says. She looks past my shoulder. "That's if I can tear her away from her new girlfriend."

"Your sister's gay?" I ask as I turn to have a look myself.

Then I see them at the table by the door, one the twin of the young woman sitting across the table from me, her red hair up in a messy bun, the other like a piece of the night that got loose and came in for a drink. Dark-haired, dark-eyed, black T-shirt and jeans. The only color is the scatter of her turquoise jewelry and she's got a lot of it.

"Corina," I say, not realizing I'm speaking her name aloud until it's out of my mouth.

"Do you know her?"

"We've met. So she and your sister are an item?"

Bess laughs. "Oh, god, no. Laurel would be horrified if she knew you'd asked that."

"She's homophobic?"

Bess keeps laughing. "No. She's just got this thing about people thinking she's gay on this trip. Women keep hitting on her."

I nod. "Listen," I say. "I've got to run a few errands."

I can see her confusion: what kind of errands does anyone run at this time of night? She probably thinks I'm a drug dealer now, but it can't be helped. I really need to avoid a run-in with Corina.

"Talk to your sister," I say. "If the pair of you decide you'd like a native guide and driver, I'll be happy to do it."

She takes the native wrong, which most people would, considering the way I look, my features and the color of my skin. Though I guess you can say I have a real claim to the term. My people saw the Indians come to this land.

"I was going to ask," she says. "What tribe do you belong to?"

"No tribe. I go my own way. Where are you staying?" I add to change the subject.

"At the Hotel Congress. It's over on —"

"I know where it is. Leave a message at the desk for me if you want to talk some more about this."

"Sure, but..."

I make a show of looking at my watch. "Shouldn't you be going back on soon?"

That draws her gaze down to her own watch. "Oh, crap. We do have to go on. And I have to rescue Laurel."

We both stand. Before I can go, she says, "You never told me your name."

"They call me Jim. Jim Changing Dog."

"They?" she asks, with a smile and a cocked eyebrow.

"Have a good set, Bess," I say.

I offer her my hand and she takes it without thinking, the way people usually do. I hold hers in mine for a longer time than would be customary, and the look in her eyes tells me she feels the same sparking energy I do.

"I really enjoyed having the chance to talk to you," I tell her.

Then I let go of her hand. To avoid walking by Corina's table, I slip out the back door on the far side of the stage that only staff are supposed to use. Sammy doesn't like me doing it, but what's he going to do? I've been coming here since the old days when the banditos used to shoot up the place. I figure I'm just making use of a grandfather clause and the rules for other customers don't apply to me.

Once I make my way out to the street, I stand there and look up at what I can see of the stars. Man, this city's grown. These days the big clear sky I remember has got a veil draped across it from all the light pollution.

I look back at the Hole and it comes to me. I didn't have to hide from Corina. Being who she is, she's got to have known I was there from the moment she came out into the courtyard herself. Probably from when she first stepped in through the front door of the Hole tonight.

Whatever she's got in mind for me, she seems to be willing to play fair and wait it out for this last couple of weeks. And if I can get that pretty little banjo player to feel the right way about me, Corina might never get her sharp coyote claws on my hide.

I half think of going back inside, but I've already made my exit. Don't want to seem too eager anyway. I'll let Bess talk it over with her sister and drop by their hotel in the morning, sweet talk them like my life depends on it. Which I suppose it does. Life as I know and want it, anyway.

So I roll myself a cigarette and get it lit, then walk the few blocks to where I parked my pickup.

It's funny. I'm courting this banjo girl so I won't get turned out into the desert where I'll have to fend for myself without any of the benefits of a human skin. But right now, all I want to do is drive out among the saguaro and spread my bedroll out in the back of my truck under the big quiet sky. Too long away, and I always get a little jumpy.

That puts a smile on my lips.

Maybe I'm more like Alice than either of us knows.

Corina

Corina pulled off the asphalt and drove her motorcycle down a dry wash, expertly maneuvering the big bike on the uneven, sandy terrain. When she was far enough from the road, she wheeled the Indian under a stand of palo verde trees and shut the engine off.

The sudden absence of the motorcycle's deep-throated motor made the subsequent quiet feel absolute until slowly the normal desert sounds returned. The rustle of rodents in the dry grass. The near-silent whisper of an owl's wings. From further away she heard the grunting of javalinas, feeding on prickly pear, while in the far distance, a coyote howled. The only response to his cry was a cluster of barks from the dogs in the nearby subdivision.

Putting the Indian up on its kickstand, Corina looked up into the branches of one of the palo verde. She'd sensed Ramona as soon as she'd pulled off the road.

"You might as well come down," she said. "I know you're up there."

"You don't always know when I'm around."

The voice was husky, sibilant on the "s" in "always."

Corina shrugged. "Like I'd care."

There was no immediate response from above, but finally there was a rustle and Ramona began her descent.

As she came down through the branches, it was hard to tell if the slithering shape belonged to a woman or a snake. It was only when she reached the ground that it became clear — at least that she was more human than reptile. She was tall and lanky, all arms and legs, with a flat chest and no hips. Her chin was sharp, light brown hair cut almost to her scalp, her eyes slanted and lidless. She wore no clothes and her skin bore a pattern of scales and diamonds like a faint tattoo.

Protruding from the end of her spine was a small rattlesnake's rattle and when she licked her lips, her tongue was darting and thin with a forked end.

"Why are you following me?" Corina asked.

"I wasn't."

"No, you just happened to show up here where I usually park my bike."

Ramona shrugged. "So maybe I was curious."

"About?"

"The red-haired girl."

"What about her?"

"Struck me she might be a cousin."

Corina nodded. "She's got a dash of deer blood, but the connection goes way back — five, maybe six generations."

"I smelled a little corn snake in her, too."

"You'd know better than me."

Ramona gave her a weary smile. "You'll never give it up, will you? Waking five-fingered beings in cousins. Waking cousins in humans. You've got all these projects, but long term or short, they never seem to work out."

"That's not true."

"It's close enough that it might as well be. When are you going to just let nature take its own course?"

Corina eyed her for a long moment. "Maybe when you start wearing clothes," she finally said, her voice dry as the cholla skeletons that littered the ground around them.

"I wear clothes," Ramona said. "I just don't like them."

"Whatever."

"You should try it a little more often." The rattlesnake woman tilted her head. "Though maybe not. Where would you put all your trinkets?"

Corina smiled. "I didn't see you at the Hole," she said to change the subject.

Hadn't smelled her either, though Ramona's scent was faint at the best of times. But that was one of her talents. Ramona could let her presence go so blank that she became invisible to all the senses. Until she moved, or she wanted you to know that she was nearby.

"I was curled up on the top of the wall," Ramona said. "Listening to the music. Have you noticed how very few people ever bother to look up? A whole world exists above their heads, but nobody ever seems to pay much attention to it."

Corina nodded. "A whole world exists all around them that most of them don't see."

"Or can't. So why bother trying to show it to them?"

"I don't know. I suppose it's in my nature."

"To meddle?"

When Corina smiled this time her teeth gleamed white and sharp in the starlight.

"I prefer to think of it as nurturing," she said.

"Well, yes, you would," Ramona told her. "Is that what you were doing? Nurturing a red-haired fiddle player?"

"I thought it was only fair...considering how Changing Dog was sniffing around her sister."

Ramona grinned. "I saw him, too. I've slept with him, you know."

Considering what the two of them were like, that was hardly a surprise. But all Corina said was, "He'll sleep with anybody who stays still long enough for him to stick it in."

"Even you?"

"He should be so lucky. But I can't really blame him. It's in his nature to sleep around — just like it's in yours to ask questions."

"So why try to change him?"

"I'm not. He has to do it for himself. And only if he wants to."

"That dog will never live up to his name."

"Maybe, maybe not. I'm only trying to wake up his spirit."

Ramona grinned. "He's got plenty of spirit."

"Not that kind," Corina said, her voice gone dry again.

"But why make him a project? He's pretty distant kin to you."

"It's just not right, cousins eating cousins. We never even considered it, back in the first days. We ate the animals that weren't cousins. And we respected them, too."

"I'm not arguing the right of that," Ramona said, "but the first days are long gone. It's getting to the point now where everybody's got some trace of the old blood in them. You could starve waiting to find someone without it."

Corina shrugged. "I know. Maybe I thought it'd help if I'd let him get to know Corn Hair, instead of just chowing down on her."

"It won't make a difference," Ramona said.

"How can you be so sure?"

"Oh, please," Ramona said. "Half the time, he's a red dog chasing down rodents in the desert. You think none of those mice and rabbits have the old blood in them? Do you think he even bothers to worry about it when those strong, handsome jaws of his are crunching their bones?"

"I don't know. But it doesn't matter. We have a bargain now."

Ramona nodded. "So what did you tell the sister he wasn't sniffing around?"

"What her mother would have told her, if she knew the way the world really turns: To be careful of the apparent kindness of strangers." Corina smiled. "And then you know what she did? She leaned across the table, gave me this long steady look, and asked, 'Does that start with you, or are you supposed to be the exception?'"

"Already I like her," Ramona said.

"What's not to like about either of them?"

Ramona nodded. "Good musicians. Sweet, innocent hearts."

"Not so innocent," Corina said. "I could tell that they've stepped out of the world before, but I don't think their experiences were quite the same. Laurel seems intrigued, ready to check out more, but the one Changing Dog was talking to — Bess. She's still carrying around some shadowy echo of the experience. I'm not sure if it's blame or shame."

"So you warned her sister about Changing Dog."

Corina shook her head. "It's not my concern if he sleeps with one or both of them. I just don't want them pulled into his game. I only told her to be careful and when she asked of what specifically, I got her talking about her music instead. She'll either think about it when Changing Dog begins his courting dance or she won't. I've done what I can."

"I'll say it again, why should you care?"

"Because when it comes to Changing Dog, I'm the one who started it. I don't want innocents caught up in his games."

"But —"

Corina cut her off. "No more questions. You're worse than a puppy."

She closed her eyes for a moment and her clothing faded away. Then she changed, woman into coyote.

"Call me kinky," Ramona said, "but there's something so sexy about the way you make the change."

Corina snapped at the hand that was reaching to pet her, then turned and loped off into the desert. Behind her, Ramona laughed quietly.

"You should try just living some time," she said. "For yourself, instead of for everybody else. You should know by now that trying to get people to change never works out."

She'd waited until the coyote was gone before she spoke, because she was tired of talking to Corina about what people should or shouldn't do. Let them make their mistakes — that was her philosophy. It made the game ever so much more interesting.

Bess

We only had to play a couple of sets, this being a weekday and all, but we made them long ones. These days we might be making a living with our music, but the one thing that hadn't changed is that we purely loved to play. If we didn't have a gig tonight, we'd still be wanting to make music somewhere. Back in our hotel room, in somebody's kitchen, out on the curb — it wouldn't matter. And I guess the audience liked what we were doing because most of the crowd stayed right until the end, even though it was a school night and most of them would have to get up to go to work in the morning.

If you're taking notes on our love life, my mysterious admirer didn't come back — yes, I looked for him — and Laurel's left right at the end of the last song we played.

It didn't take us long to pack up after our last song. We always use our own pickups and mikes, but all the rest of the gear belonged to the club and we'd been told to just leave it like it was when we were done. So it was just a matter of putting the fiddle, banjo, and guitar in their cases, the mikes, instrument cables and our songbook in our gear bag, and we were done.

Packing up right away was a habit we'd gotten into when we first started to play the roadhouses back in Tyson County. You didn't want to have some drunk come stumbling into the corner where you were set up and have him put his foot through an instrument — though that wasn't anything we had to worry about with this crowd. They'd been a little rowdy, but always in the right places, and we didn't see any fights or folks passing out on their tables the way you do back home.

I was starving and the food smelled so good I ordered us a big bowl of tortilla chips and some of the club's truly excellent salsa which we'd already sampled that afternoon when we came in to do our soundcheck. I also got myself another beer. Laurel ordered a shot of tequila and a glass of water. That's my sister for you, missing her moonshine.

We had a few people stop by our table to say nice things about the show and even buy a copy of our CD, but by the time our food came, we were on our own and I told Laurel all about Jim Changing Dog and his offer to drive us around to the other gigs we had coming up.

Laurel just smiled at me as I finished up.

"What?" I asked.

"I think you like him."

I shrugged. We couldn't hide that kind of thing from each other, and why would we want to?

"I got a good feeling from him," I said. "Like when we played that festival in Virginia and they put us in the same workshop as Jerry Douglas and Sam Bush."

"They weren't putting the moves on you."

I gave her an exasperated sigh. "I *know* they weren't. I meant the feeling good part."

Laurel laughed. "Sure you did."

I threw a tortilla chip at her but she just caught it, dipped it in the salsa and popped it into her mouth.

"So what kind of name is Changing Dog?" she asked.

"I don't know. An Indian one, I guess, though he said he didn't belong to any tribe."

"Maybe he just means he's not on the rolls. He sure looked like an Indian."

I nodded. "And did you see his eyes? They're violet."

"I didn't actually get that close a look," Laurel told me, dry humor lying in her voice. "Especially not with tall, dark and womanly making her moves on me."

"She was really hitting on you?"

"I don't know. I think maybe, but it was hard to tell."

"Jim said her name's Corina."

"Like in the Dylan song," Laurel said and hummed a couple of bars of "Corina, Corina."

I smiled. "You're just filled up with useful information."

"Like you didn't think the same thing."

I hadn't, actually. Too busy enjoying Jim's company, I guess.

"So how does he know her?" Laurel asked.

"He didn't say."

"Well, she was pretty darn intense. And she kept acting like she was warning me about something, but when I'd ask her what, she'd just change the subject."

"Weird."

"Umm. But she knows her music — old-timey and seventies. She knew exactly which Clash song we lifted for that bridge we've been sticking in the middle of 'Uncle Cloony Played the Banjo,' plus she knew exactly who Alan Munde was."

I was impressed. Most of our fans would know either one or the other.

"So did you ask for a bracelet?"

"As if," she said and kicked at me under the table, but I was expecting it and had already moved my leg.

I gave her an innocent look that wouldn't fool anybody. "I just thought you might have traded for a CD."

"I should trade you."

"For more than a bracelet, I hope."

"I didn't notice Mr. Violet Eyes wearing any," she said. "Of course I wasn't leaning across the table, fluttering my lashes at him."

"He does have nice eyes," I said, remembering.

"So tell me more about him."

"I don't know what there is to tell. He was easy to talk to. Kind of flirty, but not in an icky way. He sort of reminded me of that guy from up past Hickory Holler that Adie used to date. You know, as in he's a genuine hardass, but he also has a real heart of gold under his bad boy finish."

"He acted like a tough?"

I shook my head. "I'm not explaining it right. He didn't act like that at all. But you just *knew* he was tough."

"So do you think we should take him up on his offer?" Laurel asked.

"Well, it'd save us a pile of money. And it'd be great to have somebody local show us around."

"Plus you'd get to hang with him."

"Big plus."

Laurel pursed her lips, thinking. "I don't know. That's a lot of lonesome country we'd be driving through."

"I thought of that, too. But I get a good feeling from him."

Laurel grinned.

"Not that kind of good feeling," I said. "Well, maybe. I just meant, I think we can trust him."

"Except maybe Corina was warning me about him."

That made me think about how, during the break, Jim had looked over to where Laurel and Corina were sitting. Two seconds later and he was out of his chair and saying good-bye.

"I don't think he cared much for her," I said. I hesitated a moment, then added, "I think maybe she even made him a little nervous."

"I knew it. He's a serial killer and my dark-haired admirer was trying to warn us about him. But she's too frightened to come right out and say anything, because she knows that then she'll be next."

"Laurel."

"I'm kidding."

"Besides," I said. *"He* seemed nervous about *her."*

"Because he knows that she can reveal all his deep, dark secrets."

"Laurel."

"I'm *kidding."*

"He seemed really nice."

"And hot."

"In a cowboyish way."

"Which," Laurel said, grinning, "is not at all a bad thing."

"If you like cowboys."

"Which you always have."

I just laughed. She could *so* get me going.

"I think you should meet him and see for yourself," I said. "Then we can decide."

"Did you make plans to see him again?"

I shook my head. "He just said to leave him a message at the front desk of the hotel."

"Where we should be going," Laurel said.

She tipped her tequila glass up to her mouth, but it was already empty. Giving me a sad look, she licked the rim of the glass, then set it down and stood up.

"I'll see about calling us a cab," she said.

I nodded, but I was only half paying attention because I was busy thinking about Jim's eyes again, and the promises I'd seen in them.

I keep my promises, he'd told me.

I wasn't sure if that'd be a good or a bad thing, but it didn't stop me from getting a warm, wriggly feeling deep inside.

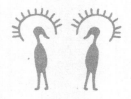

Once Upon a Time in Tucson

Alice Corn Hair

ALICE LEFT THOMAS sleeping in their bedroom. She had a shower and made some coffee, then slipped out of the house, heading for the trailhead at the end of the road that ran along the back of Thomas's property — *their* property, Thomas would say, but even after living as long as she had in the human world, Alice still had trouble thinking of the land as something that anyone could own.

A red-tailed hawk hung in the sky, watching her as she walked along the dusty road. She smiled and waved to it.

"Hello, brother!" she called.

The hawk might have dipped his wings in reply. Or he might have only been adjusting to a change in the thermal he rode. It didn't matter. Alice never expected a response from her wild cousins, not when she was in human form herself.

She wasn't sure they even recognized her, a five-fingered being walking in the desert on two legs, but it was in human shape that she was best able to follow the teachings of the *curanderas* and the other wise women who had set her on her spiritual path — the road that connected her to her own medicine. Coming to her teachers as a woman had allowed her to speak to them on an equal footing, rather than being viewed as some all-knowing spirit guide.

The one gap in the vast wealth of knowledge that the *curanderas* passed from one to another was the simple fact that the animal people weren't all guides; many of them needed mentors and direction as much as any human did. The wiser teachers were rightly wary of the evil beings and trickster spirits that could lead you astray. But they, too, seemed unaware that many animal people were as uninformed in the old wisdoms as novice humans, and following their advice could just as easily put you in danger.

And everyone had advice to share — that didn't change from one world to another. From the drunk in the trailer park, barely able to string two coherent words together, to the university professor in his wood-paneled study hall. From the punky-feathered phainopepla with his beak full of berries, to the roundtail ground squirrel bathing in the sun. Everyone had advice and bad advice was bad advice, sometimes merely distracting, other times outright dangerous. Whether it originated in nasty intentions or ignorance didn't change the unhappy results that could arise from following it.

Human form had other benefits for the spiritual road she followed. It allowed her to sketch and collect the herbs and healing plants she used in her studies. To weave baskets, bead medicine bags, and make the smudge sticks she used in her private ceremonies. It was impossible to sew on beads or light a smudge stick with a jackalope's paws.

The hawk caught her attention again as he dropped from the sky to perch on the tall aerial that rose from one of the neighboring houses.

It was going to be another hot day, Alice thought as she looked away from him.

The desert was full of surprises, but the rising temperatures going into the summer months wasn't one of them. Alice liked the dry, baking heat. Not enough to go out in the middle of the day without a hat and a bottle of water, but she didn't need the AC in the house. That was for Thomas, who began to wilt once it got over eighty. A bit of shade at the hottest part of the day was the most she required.

She smiled, thinking of Thomas, but that made her think of Changing Dog and how in a little under two weeks she was going to lose her husband, lose everything when Coyote Woman took away her ability to wear human skin. Alice's smile faded. She would still be able to follow the medicine road, but it would be harder without human hands, or a human voice. And she would have to walk it on her own. She couldn't expect Thomas to live with a jackalope, never mind love one.

He knew what she was. Often when he painted her it was as a human woman, but with antlers and the long ears of a jackrabbit, the half-shape she wore when she strayed into the borderlands between this world and the spirit world, what her Yaqui teachers called *huya aniya*. He accepted her exotic origins in that quiet, gentle way he accepted everything in the world. But if she couldn't come to his bed as his lover anymore? If they couldn't talk, or hold hands, or...

Distracted by her thoughts, she didn't notice Changing Dog's truck parked at the trailhead until she was almost upon it. Changing Dog leaned against the door of the truck, smoking a cigarette. He pushed away from the vehicle when he saw he had her attention, that big easy smile of his stretching his lips.

Alice was neither happy nor unhappy to see him. Changing Dog was like a family's black sheep — always getting into some sort of trouble, always with a scheme in mind. She wished he wasn't so likeable. It would be so much easier to simply ignore him. Though allowing themselves to ignore each other hadn't been part of Coyote Woman's plan, whatever that plan was. Alice had given up worrying at the riddle of it a long time ago.

"You're up early," she said.

Changing Dog shrugged. "Maybe I've changed my ways. Like the leopard changing his stripes."

"Spots."

He grinned. "Botany was never my strong suit."

Alice held back from correcting him again now that she realized that he was only trying to get a rise out of her. She watched him put his cigarette out under the heel of his boot, then pocket the butt.

"So are you going for a hike?" she asked.

"No, I was waiting for you."

"I think we've talked it out as much as we're ever going to."

Changing Dog shook his head. "It's not like that. I've met this girl."

"A girl."

"She's amazing. Beautiful. A musician."

"Where did you meet her?"

"She and her sister were playing at the Hole last night." He grinned. "And I think she likes me."

"That's a good start," Alice said.

Changing Dog nodded. "Except things being the way they are, we don't have a whole lot of time."

That was an understatement, Alice thought. But if anyone could get someone to fall in love with them in the time they did have, it would be Changing Dog.

"So I was wondering," he said, "if you could use that *brujería* of yours to make me some kind of love potion or spell."

Alice sighed. "You know it doesn't work that way."

"So you don't know how to make one."

"I didn't say that. But I don't agree with them on general principle, and I particularly don't agree with the idea of using one for this. The person you find has to love you unconditionally — of her *own* volition. Not because you tricked her into it."

"I think she will love me," Changing Dog said. "In time. But we're running out of time. You said so yourself the other night. So I just want to hurry up what's going to come on its own anyway."

"I appreciate your making the effort. Really I do. But this isn't the way."

"Who's going to know?"

"Coyote Woman."

He shook his head. *"How* would she know? Neither of us are going to tell her."

"She's Coyote Woman. How could she *not* know?"

Changing Dog said nothing for a long moment. He rolled himself another cigarette and lit it without offering her one.

"I'm really trying here," he said finally.

Too little, too late, Alice thought, but she only nodded.

"And if this doesn't work out," he went on, "the only other option is you and me."

Alice shook her head. "That's not going to happen."

"Why not? Is it a cross-species thing? Because that doesn't cut it. Hell, even Cody's got himself a magpie girlfriend. If an old coyote like him can get together with a corbæ, why can't you look past my red fur?"

"It's not like that."

But Changing Dog wasn't listening. "They're canid and magpie," he said, "and they're getting along just fine. A red dog and a jackalope isn't any bigger of a stretch."

Alice shook her head. "It's not that I don't care about you. It's that I love Thomas."

"So you'd rather give everything up? It's got to be all or nothing?"

"No, but it has to be true."

Changing Dog sighed. "I don't even know what that word means. Everybody's got their own idea about what's true and what isn't."

"I suppose they do. I mean it has to feel right inside me." She laid a hand on her breast. "In here, I know the difference. And I'm sure you do, too."

Changing Dog didn't reply immediately. He looked out across the desert and blew a stream of grey-blue smoke into the air. Long moments passed before he turned back to look at her.

"I don't know what I know," he said.

He ground his cigarette out under his boot, then bent down and picked up the butt.

"Changing Dog," Alice said as he started to turn away.

"I've got a human name, too, Corn Hair."

He put the butt in the pocket of his jean jacket and walked over to his truck.

"Jim," she said.

He got in the cab and looked at her.

"We've got a couple of weeks left," he said. "Enjoy them."

He started up the truck before she could reply, then drove off, leaving her with the plumes of dust thrown up by his wheels as he pulled away from the trailhead.

She watched until he was lost from sight, understanding how he felt. She understood all too well. But wasn't it so typical of him to wait until the last moment before making an effort.

Finally she turned back to where the trail began, hoping that the desert could help her calm the fear that had found its own permanent lodging in her heart.

"Live life like a ceremony," one of her first teachers had told her. "Take responsibility for your every breath. Be aware of all the wide wonder of the world that surrounds you and connects the thing you are to every other thing."

"You mean all the time?"

"Would that be such a chore?"

"It's just...when do you relax?"

The old woman smiled. "Who says it's not relaxing?"

Alice sighed now, remembering. It was true. It seemed hard at first, but eventually it became as natural as breathing. But the trouble was, heightened awareness included a heightened sense of who and what and where she was in the complex pattern that made up the world. Today, that knowledge only served as a constant reminder of their upcoming meeting with Coyote Woman.

She wished she could just have an empty head instead. That she could be aware of nothing.

She heard a sharp *kee-ahrrr* in the sky and looked up to see a hawk like the one she'd greeted earlier. For no good reason, the wild presence of him floating there, high above her, lifted her spirits.

Nothing had changed.

Her world as she'd known it was still ending.

But that, she realized as she followed the trail that wound its way in between the towering saguaro cacti, was all the more reason to appreciate what she had now, while she still had it.

Bess

"Do me up like I'm you," I said the next morning before we went down to the Cup Café for breakfast.

We were enjoying our stay at the Hotel Congress. I wasn't enamored with the dance music coming from the club downstairs while we were trying to sleep, or the radio blaring up from what I assumed was the kitchen way too early in the morning, but neither bothered Laurel, and the hotel definitely ranked among the cooler places we've stayed. The big lobby immediately set the tone, kind of Southwest bangs up against Art Deco. It had a tile floor, high ceilings with the wooden rafters showing, tan plaster walls decorated with brightly-colored, Southwestern pictograph designs, lots of old wood and iron banisters, a wide stairway going to the rooms upstairs, an actual retro telephone booth, an art show hung on the walls...oh, and a piano: a nice upright Meister, what they call a cabinet grand. Before we even checked in, Laurel had to sit down and play "Wildwood Flower" on it — the only song she knows all the way through on the piano.

The clerk who checked us in had purple hair and about as much hardware on his face as you'd find in the back of Sweeney's General Store back home. Everything was pierced, usually more than once. Which was cool. Most places we can afford to stay in seem to get their desk clerks from some big, generic, trailer park gene pool and they couldn't care less whether we're coming or going, just so long as we can pay our bill. This guy not only had a great look, but he never stopped grinning and chatting with us — which is how I saw the three studs piercing his tongue.

We asked for a room on the top floor and he told us that they were missing the third floor — apparently the Feds burned it down to smoke out John Dillinger, a guest at the time — so would a room on the second do? What were we supposed to say? Laurel just smiled and leaned on the counter, telling him, "I do like a place with a little history."

By the time we left the desk, I'm sure he was half in love with her. No surprise, there. I'm her sister and she enchants me just as much as she does pretty much everyone else she meets.

She grinned at me now from the bathroom where she was drying her hair with a towel.

"What are you up to?" she asked.

"I just want to see something."

I didn't have to say what. She knew. We're identical twins, but we're not identical people. Laurel likes to dress up more than I do. She wears more makeup. Her hair behaves better for her because she takes more time pampering it. Those are the quick recognition cues that people who don't really know us will usually use to tell us apart.

So when we want to mess with someone, I get Laurel to do her makeup on me and tame my hair a little. She musses her hair up, puts on the touch of lipstick I wear, we swap clothes, and you'd be surprised how many people can't tell the difference. Or maybe you wouldn't. We're pretty good at acting like each other, too.

"I tried the fairy tale question on Jim," I said as she was doing my eyes.

"So what did he say?"

"Yes. A big, emphatic yes."

Laurel stepped back, the mascara applicator in her hand. "Really?"

I nodded, understanding her surprise. We asked people that question all the time, but no one ever answered it right. By "right" I mean, that you could tell they really believed — instead of them being kind of wacky, or trying to get into our pants and they'd say anything they thought might get the zipper down faster. So far the only people we knew who could answer it properly were our sisters. And maybe Mama, though I'm pretty sure she only believes because we all do.

It's more of a Laurel thing than mine. Truth is, I'd just as soon forget our own close encounter with the fairy kind. But I went along with it when she first said we should ask people and by now it had become a habit. I hadn't really thought about it much until Jim actually said, yes, he did believe.

"So then what happened?" Laurel asked.

I shrugged. "Nothing. I didn't get into it then. It didn't seem like the right time or place."

"And he didn't want to know why you asked?"

"No. He seems..." I wasn't sure how to put it. "It's like he lives sideways to the world, if that makes any sense. I kept feeling like he's a piece of a secret and I didn't want to talk about our own experiences because I wasn't sure how much I wanted to know about his."

"And this is the guy you want to drive around in the desert with?"

"I don't think he's dangerous. Or at least, I don't think he'd be dangerous for us."

"Just how much do you like this guy anyway?" Laurel asked as she went back to working on my eyes.

I can't believe she goes through all this preparation once a day. Usually more than once.

"I don't know," I said. "Probably too much for someone I've just met."

"Well, maybe Corina — hold still!" she said as I started to sit up straighter, a retort already forming on my lips. "What I was going to say," she went on, "is that maybe Corina wasn't talking about Jim when she was giving me her vague warning, but that doesn't mean you shouldn't be careful all the same."

"I know."

"And..?"

"I don't think I care."

Laurel smiled. "Now I've got to meet him."

⊟ ⊟ ⊟

I left a message at the front desk on the way to the entrance of the Cup Café a little further down the lobby — not saying that we'd take Jim up on his offer, just that Laurel would like to meet him — then we went in and found seats by the window where we could look out at the patio and the street beyond. It was another of those beautiful days I imagined they must get most of the time around here. Warm and sunny, the sky so blue above the building across the street it didn't feel real.

"Ellie would love the light in this place," Laurel said.

I nodded. Ellie was the artist in our family, although Grace was showing some talent in that direction. She might even get as good as Ellie, if she and her twin Ruth could ever stop playing the fool every chance they got.

When the waitress finally came, we ordered the strongest coffee they had along with a couple of orders of toast and jam. We were on our second cup each when Jim sauntered into the café, looking even better in the daylight than he had in the courtyard of the Hole last night. It's not that he's handsome, so much as completely present, if that makes any sense. He totally inhabits himself, which most people don't. When you do see somebody so comfortable in their own skin, it stands out.

And then there are those violet eyes...

Well, we already knew that he'd passed the fairy tale question with flying colors. And as he came up to our table, he passed the next test, too, because he looked right at me and said, "Hello, Bess," before he turned to Laurel, adding, "And you must be Laurel."

"How could you tell?" Laurel asked. "You don't even know us."

"Your energy signatures are different."

"Energy signatures." Laurel's voice held a touch of humor.

He shrugged. "I could have said 'vibe,' but that sounds so retro."

"It's okay. We like retro."

"Do you want to sit with us and have a coffee?" I asked. "Though it might be awhile before we can get the waitress to come back to our table to take your order."

He smiled. "Half the time this place runs on Indian time. I'll go get one myself."

Laurel turned in her chair to watch him as he went to the counter where the waitress was talking on a cell phone.

"Yum," she said.

I nodded. "So now you understand."

"Completely. I just wish I'd seen him first."

"And disappoint Corina?"

I didn't move my leg quickly enough and she got me on the shin. Luckily she was wearing high tops today so it didn't hurt.

Laurel added her patented fake sweet smile to the kick. "You know what Mama says."

I knew. We weren't responsible for what other people wanted from us, only for what we did ourselves. I figure it was the advice that got her through Granny Burrell's endless pestering about her getting a new father for us girls.

"I'm just teasing," I said.

"Well, it's getting old," Laurel told me, but she smiled. "So," she added, leaning closer to me across the table. "How do you want to handle *your* admirer? Do I give him the third degree, or do we just talk?"

"Your call," I said.

I looked up and smiled at Jim as he returned to the table, coffee in one hand, a plateful of muffins in the other. He set them all down before pulling out a chair and sitting down with us.

"Somebody's hungry," Laurel said.

"I brought them to share."

"Thanks, they look good," I said and helped myself to one that looked like it had cranberries in it.

"So what have you two done so far?" Jim asked.

The question confused me. "In our lives?"

He laughed. "No, I meant in Tucson. You didn't tell me when you got into town and I was wondering if you'd had a chance to take in any of the sights."

"We walked down to Fourth Avenue," Laurel said. "But we spent so long in that big thrift shop that we only got to window shop the other stores."

"I was thinking of something less commercial."

"Like what?"

"Like the desert. You up for a hike?"

"What's to see in the desert?" I asked.

He smiled. "You'd be surprised."

So we ended up talking about the various hikes we could take and by the time we paid our bill, it had been decided that Laurel and I were going up to our room to change into what we could put together as hiking gear. We never did get around to talking about who Jim was and what he did.

But, "I like him," Laurel said as we went up the stairs. "And I see what you mean about him living inside a secret. You just look into those gorgeous eyes and a world of mystery seems to enfold around you."

"Not to mention promises."

Laurel laughed. "I think he's saving those for you."

Ramona

"It's not that people don't like snakes," Ramona said, "it's that they don't understand them."

She wasn't sure how they'd gotten onto the topic, but all things considered, she had strong opinions on it and wasn't about to let it go now. Of course, Ramona tended to have strong opinions on whatever was being discussed.

"So that's your theory?" Jorge asked.

Ramona nodded. "And I'm sticking to it."

They were sitting on an outcrop of red stone overlooking Gates Pass Boulevard as it cut through the Tucson Mountains west of the city. From this vantage they had a decent view of Avra Valley beyond the pass, Tucson, spread out on the other side of the mountains, and the road below that wound through the rocks, connecting the two.

In deference to all the five-fingered beings walking around with their *tourista* cameras and holiday smiles, Ramona looked about as human as she ever got. Still tall and lanky-lean, but her eyes had lids now, her skin was an even reddish brown. Her tongue, when she licked her lips, was rounded and soft. She was wearing clothes, too: a white tank top and baggy shorts with what seemed like a half-hundred pockets — just like so many of the *touristas*. Only she was barefoot and her hair was still cropped close enough to her scalp so as to be no more than a vague promise.

Her companion was a javalina when he wasn't in human shape. Sitting with her now he was a broad-shouldered, dark-skinned man with short arms and legs, dressed in loose white cotton trousers and T-shirt, with a beaded leather vest overtop. His hair was a stiff, grizzled grey buzzcut, his face almost split in two by a large white handlebar moustache. He exuded a faint musky odor — faint, at least, compared to when he was in his cousin shape — that turned heads when other hikers went by.

"Well, I've never had a problem with snakes," he said. "I don't have a problem with anybody, so long as they leave me alone."

"You weren't asking to be left alone a few nights ago."

He laughed. "Anytime, *chica*. When it's you, the pleasure's always mine."

He took a drink from the water bottle he was carrying and offered it to her. Ramona smiled her thanks and drank as well, her gaze on the road below. Something caught her eye and she sat up. A trickle of water escaped the bottle as she took it away from her lips, dribbling down onto the front of her T-shirt, but she paid it no mind.

"Was that Changing Dog's truck I just saw go by?" she asked.

Jorge didn't even bother to look, but he nodded. "With those two pretty red-haired girls you were telling me about riding shotgun."

"So he's going for both of them."

"Going how?"

"Oh, you know. We're getting close up on the end of one of those stories of Corina's."

Jorge nodded, remembering. "So he has — what? A couple of months left to work it out?"

"More like two weeks."

"If anyone can do it, that red dog can. I've never seen a cousin so lucky with the *muchachas.*"

But Ramona wasn't listening to him.

"This isn't good," she said. "Those girls are too young and impressionable. One, hell, both of them could easily fall in love with him."

Jorge smiled. "He's an inspiration, all right."

"No, you don't get it," Ramona told him. "It's not supposed to happen. He's supposed to go to Corina empty-handed, just the way he started this two-legged life of his."

"And why would that be?" Jorge asked, his voice patient.

"Because if he succeeds, it'll just encourage Corina to keep interfering in people's lives."

"What's it to you?"

"Nothing. Everything."

"This have anything to do with the cowboy you were seeing last fall?"

It was months ago now, but it still rankled. Meddling Corina, deciding that Billy should get in touch with his bighorn blood. He woke quickly and too well, and couldn't handle the Rattlesnake Woman he discovered his lover to be. Who knew a big strong cowboy like that could be so afraid of snakes?

Ramona hadn't been in love with him, exactly. It hadn't even had the potential to be close to long-term. But the way it worked was, Ramona decided when a relationship ended. Nobody walked out on *her*. Or rather, went scrambling out the door like the very fact of her existence was a nightmare.

"Of course it's got something to do with Billy," she told Jorge. "Was I supposed to just forget something like that?"

Jorge gave a slow shake of his head. "So what are you going to do?"

"I don't know. I'll think of something. Maybe I'll get those twin sisters to see Changing Dog's worst side." She grinned. "Even if I have to make it up. And if that doesn't work, I suppose I can always keep them too busy to fall in love with him by turning them against each other." She nodded to herself. "That shouldn't be too hard. What family ever gets along?"

"Mine does."

"That's different. You come from herding stock."

She meant no ill by the term, though some of the cousins would take offense. The predators among them often used it as an insult, mistaking the closeness of the family units as a weakness.

Jorge took the comment at face value, as a simple statement of fact.

"I thought you said they had red deer in them," he said.

"They do. But they also have a touch of snake, so I'll play on that."

"You didn't say they were your kin."

Ramona shrugged. "Very distant. The blood's so weak I can't tell whose it was originally."

She got up, shading her eyes to see where the truck was going.

"You know this isn't so different from what Corina does," Jorge said.

"It's completely different."

Jorge shrugged. "<Ah well,>" he said in Spanish. "<You're all crazy women, anyway.>"

"<I understand Spanish,>" Ramona told him in the same language.

"I know you do."

She went back to following the pickup with her gaze. "He's probably taking them sightseeing. To the Desert Museum, or maybe one of the trails. I'm going to have a closer look." She turned to Jorge. "Are you coming?"

"It's a beautiful day," he said. "The sun is warm and there are plenty of pretty little *touristas* to look at. I don't think so."

"Suit yourself."

She started to hand the water bottle back to him, but he shook his head.

"Keep it."

"Thanks," she said.

Then she turned and continued up the side of the red rock pass, planning to go cross-country to where she guessed Changing Dog was taking the red-haired twins. As soon as she was out of sight of the tourists and hikers, she stepped into *el entre,* the borderland that lay between the spiritworld and this one. It was a place where time moved at a different pace, sometimes faster, sometimes slower, depending on where you were in it. There she could move more quickly, actually getting ahead of Changing Dog's pickup.

By the time the vehicle was passing the Desert Museum on Kinney Road, she was in the scrub under a pair of tall saguaro, watching it go by. She popped back into *el entre,* emerging in time to see them also passing the Red Hills Visitors' Center. She moved back and forth between *el entre* a few more times, following the pickup as it continued down Kinney and turned up Hohokam Road, before she was finally rewarded by seeing it pull into the parking lot of the Sendero Esperanza trailhead.

She waited to be sure that they would actually take the trail, then moved into *el entre* one more time so that she could be waiting for them where the Sendero Esperanza trail crosses the Hugh Norris. She would look up in surprise from where she was sitting under the shade of a tall red rock, her feet dangling just above a stand of prickly pear, a tall saguaro leaning close as though listening to some secret she had to tell it.

Jim

I love watching people the first time they're in the desert, when they're actually walking among the aunts and uncles and can have firsthand experience of the diversity of life to be found here.

Most people's impression of this land is that it's all empty. That there's nothing here. But to me they're the most beautiful places in the world, full of life and spirit, and the Sonoran Desert around Tucson's pretty much a crown jewel. It's not the biggest or most dramatic stretch of badlands you'll ever encounter in your life, but I'll argue that it's got the most heart. Of course I'm biased; this is the land that gave me birth and has nourished me for all these years.

I know that what it has to offer isn't necessarily going to appeal to everyone. I've met people who just see dust, rocks, ugly plants, and uglier wildlife. And since Bess and Laurel come from a landscape that's about as green as it gets, I couldn't be sure that they'd appreciate it. But I had to try.

I know for sure that they aren't too impressed with the rust bucket that passes for my truck. It's a '57 Ford and you can only guess at the original color under the patina of rust, primer, and the various patches of paint that connect them.

They're both nervous as soon as I pull out of the Hotel Congress's parking lot into the traffic, and it only gets worse when we take Speedway out of the city and start climbing into the Tucsons on Gates Pass Boulevard. But I guess they know vehicles and come to realize that this truck has a good heart and I know how to drive it, because after awhile they start to relax. And once we get high enough into the pass and the view of the Avra Valley on the other side of the mountains opens up for us, well, they both sigh with pleasure.

Laurel's in the shotgun seat, with Bess in between us, and I like that. The jostle of her leg or her shoulder against mine as we take a curve sets little sparks going through me. And now, with that view filling her gaze, she kind of leans against me with this happy grin on her face, and that feels even better.

I'm tempted to take them to the Desert Museum — it's a great place to get an overview of what the desert's all about — but it's not real. The museum tries hard, and I appreciate that most of the animals they have on display are ones that have been taken in because of injuries and couldn't survive in the wild, but it's still too much like a prison for me. Or a rehab unit.

So I drive on past, heading north until I finally pull into the parking lot of the Sendero Esperanza trailhead and shut off the engine.

"So what do you think so far?" I ask them.

"I just want to know why they call it a desert," Laurel says. "I mean, everywhere you look, there's something growing. Even flowers. I never expected to see flowers out here."

Bess just gives me another grin.

"Spring's the wildflower season," I tell Laurel. "A result of the February rains. But it's funny. We had the rain this year, but we're not getting the usual displays."

"And the desert part?" she asks.

"It's a technical thing, I guess. Something to do with the amount of rainfall a place gets."

"Well, it's not the Sahara."

I laugh. "No. But I'll bet the Sahara's got its high points, too."

When we get out of the truck I start to give them a little talk about being careful around some of the cacti and the like, but Laurel cuts me off.

"It's okay," she says. "It's not like we've never been out hiking. We grew up in the country. Just to visit our sister it's an hour's walk in the hills behind our farm."

So I shrug and I don't even tell her "I told you so" when she takes a shortcut across one loop of the trail, starts to slide and ends up with a handful of thorns from a cholla cactus that she grabbed to break her fall.

"This is so weird," she says as I pick out the thorns with the tweezers I stuck in my pocket before we left the truck. "Back home when we go climbing, we just naturally grab on to whatever's closest to hand to help us up."

"Well, you can't do that here," I tell them. "Everything's got a thorn. And be careful about picking up rocks and things. You'll never know what little critters you might startle from under it and we've got some dangerous ones. Scorpions. Spiders. Snakes."

"We've got snakes back home," Laurel says. She looks at Bess. "Remember Aunt Lillian's story about when she got snake bit?"

"Aunt Lillian had the best stories," Bess agrees.

Laurel's pretty good as I take out the little barbed thorns. She grimaces, but doesn't cry or make a sound. She and Bess just chat away like this is some everyday thing and they both go up in my estimation. I like a woman with some toughness bred into her.

I finally get the last thorn out and we continue on up the trail, Laurel sticking with us now, though still walking ahead. A red-tailed hawk accompanies us for awhile. We spot a couple of cactus wrens and a whole mess of lizards — little brown and grey cousins. Bess keeps trying to get a picture of them, but they won't hold their poses for her. I wait until I spot another and then call her over.

"Wait," I say as she starts to creep up on it. I turn back to the lizard. "Let's be polite, cousin," I tell it. "Nobody's going to hurt you. All she wants to do is take your picture, show everybody back home how handsome you are. So what do you say?"

It studies my face for a long moment and I smile, waving Bess over.

"No sudden moves," I tell her, "but I think he'll hold that pose long enough for you to get a picture."

He does, and she does. And then he darts away among the scrub and rocks.

"How'd you do that?" Bess asks.

I shrug. "I can get along with most anybody — so long as I'm not hungry."

"You'd *eat* a lizard?"

"I've eaten worse. But not today."

"Why'd you call him 'cousin,'" Laurel wants to know.

I give another shrug. "Well, we're all family, aren't we?"

That earns me a puzzled look from both of them.

"I guess," Laurel says.

A little further up the trail, she looks back over her shoulder at us and points to the closest saguaro, an old giant, towering some thirty feet above us, with a whole crown of side arms coming out of the main trunk at about twenty feet up.

"I love these cacti," she says. "They're like you always see in the cartoons when the characters are in the desert."

"But they're so much more beautiful than a cartoon," Bess says.

Her sister nods. "Totally. And they've got so much personality."

"The Tohono O'odham call them the uncles and the aunts," I tell them.

Bess smiles. "I like that. It gives them a friendly sound."

"The way they tell the story," I go on, "is that if you live a good life, you come back as a saguaro."

"And if you live a bad one?" Bess asks, playing the straight man for me.

I smile. "You come back as a five-fingered being. A human."

"That's a funny expression," Laurel says. "'Five-fingered being'."

I shrug and hold out my hands, wiggling my fingers.

"It's what sets us apart from the animals," I say.

That earns me another odd look from Laurel. I get the feeling that she's got something more to say, but then she just shrugs and takes the lead again.

The Sendero Esperanza trail's not particularly strenuous, but it's still four winding miles uphill to the top ridge west of Amole peak. From there you can take the Hugh Norris trail on up to Wassan Peak, the highest point of the Tucsons. But I'm only aiming to bring us as far as the ridge today. You get a spectacular view from here, on both sides of the mountains. I like the southwestern view best, looking down on the saguaro forest that grows up out of a granite-strewn landscape from the Tucsons all the way to the Baboquivari Mountains, south and west of the Avra Valley.

We're not alone on the trail. Occasionally we pass other hikers and when we get to the top I spot a familiar figure. I think for a moment that she's waiting for us, but then I have to laugh at myself. How would Ramona know to come looking for us up here?

"Hey, Jim," she says as we get closer. Her gaze travels to the twins. "I see you finally got yourself a pair of red-haired girls. Twins, too. Nice going."

Laurel looks from her to me. "What's that supposed to mean?"

"Don't pay her any mind," I say. "That's just Ramona. She'll say any damn thing that pops into her mind if she thinks it'll get a rise out of you."

"Oh, right," Ramona says. "Like you haven't had a hard-on for a threesome since just about forever." She looks back at the twins. "'And I want 'em red-haired,' he'd say, ''cos the red-haired ones can go all night.'" She laughs. "Course we all know that old Changing Dog himself has no trouble keeping it up as long as you want it."

I shake my head. "Shut up," I tell her, but the damage is already done.

Bess moves away from me, over to where Laurel is standing, and I don't like the look in their eyes. I don't know what Ramona's game is — hell, she doesn't need a reason to cause mischief — but she gives us all a leering grin, then slips off the stone where she's lounging.

"You all have fun now," she says and then she saunters off, lean hips swinging.

There's a long silence as we watch her head down the trail. I can pretty much guess what the twins are thinking. Me? I'm planning on a rattlesnake hunt once I get them back to town.

"Do you know her?" Bess finally asks.

My gaze slowly tracks back to her face, not wanting to see the hurt there.

"Everybody knows her," I say. "You look up 'trouble' in a dictionary and they usually have a picture of her on the page."

"No, I meant...is she like a girlfriend or something?"

I shake my head. "But we've been intimate. The result of bad tequila and worse judgment."

"I think maybe we should go back to town," she says. Her disappointment in me's pretty plain to see, but it's the hurt in her eyes that makes my chest go tight. "I mean, this is too weird."

Laurel nods. "I'll say."

"I really thought you were nicer," Bess says to me. "That it wasn't just a sex thing."

Laurel turns to look at her sister. "What sex thing?"

"What that woman was saying."

Laurel actually laughs.

"Oh for god's sake, Bess," she says. "She was so obviously ragging on him."

"But...then what did you think was weird?"

"The way she was totally checking me out." Laurel looks at me. "You saw that, right?"

I give a slow nod, not sure where this is going.

"You know I'm not homophobic," Laurel says. "Honestly. I love women. I just don't want to have sex with them. How does that make me homophobic?"

"It doesn't," I say.

"Exactly. I mean, is it too much to ask for just one hunky guy to be attracted to me on this tour?"

Bess is still looking at me, but the hurt look's not in her eyes anymore. The corners of her mouth are even twitching.

"I'm sure there are lots," she tells her sister. "They're just the shy ones this time around."

But Laurel isn't listening. "I know we're different people, but we look the same, right? So what makes them gather around you and ignore me?"

"Nobody's ignoring —"

"It's giving me an inferiority complex. What is it? Am I putting out some kind of pheromone that tells men to back off? And attracts women?"

"Would you look at the view," I say.

Laurel turns to me, a bit of fire in her eyes, then she just laughs and has a look.

"It's gorgeous," she says. "And we're idiots to be standing around talking about all of this on such a beautiful day, in such a beautiful place."

Bess nods and comes over to where I'm standing. She hooks her arm in the crook of mine.

"I'm sorry," she says. "It was just...weird."

I nod. "That's Ramona for you."

"I mean, it's not like I don't have my own history, with guys that could be just as strange."

"I hope not as strange as her."

Bess smiles. "So it was a bad breakup?"

"There was nothing to break up. We were out at a party, there was too much tequila, and the next morning we woke up together. It wasn't something either of us had planned — I don't think I'm her type, and she's sure not mine. We had breakfast and carried on with our lives. I've seen her a dozen times since then and she's never seemed even vaguely interested in getting together again, so I don't know what all of that was about, except Ramona creating a little drama."

Laurel turned from the view for a moment. "Maybe she likes you more than you think."

"Maybe," I say. "But the feeling isn't mutual."

Bess gives my arm a squeeze. "Here's our Mama's advice on this kind of thing: We're not responsible for what other people want from us, only for what we do ourselves."

"That's good advice."

"What kind of birds are those?" Laurel asks.

I look up to where she's pointing to see a dozen or more buzzards doing slow circles above us.

"Turkey buzzards," I say. "They're waiting for us to fall down and die so that they can have their dinner."

"Well that's not going to happen!" Laurel calls up to them.

I decide to put off the rattlesnake hunt I had planned to undertake after I'd dropped the twins back at their hotel. I don't know what Ramona was up to, but whatever it was, it backfired, because on the hike back down to the parking lot, we're getting along better than ever. We watch the sunset from the low hills at the Ez-kim-in-zin picnic area across the Golden Gate Road from the trailhead, then I take them over to one of my favorite out-of-the-way restaurants, El Pitayo on Sandario Road, before we make the long drive back through the mountains and down into Tucson again.

When we get to the hotel, Laurel goes on ahead inside, but Bess lingers with me for a moment beside the pickup.

"I had a great time today," she says. "It's so different being in a place like this when you've got someone to show you around."

"I had a great time, too."

"So are you busy tomorrow?" she asks. "Or am I being too forward? My sister Adie says guys don't like pushy girls."

"Your sister's wrong," I assure her. "At least so far as I'm concerned. And my day's yours."

"See you for breakfast?"

I nod.

She presses up against me and lifts her head for a kiss. By the time she pulls away, I'm feeling a little dizzy. I don't know what this woman has, exactly, but she's got me feeling things I've never felt before.

She gives me another kiss, drops a hand to my buttocks and gives them a squeeze. She's grinning when she steps back.

"See you tomorrow," she says.

"I don't know that I can wait that long," I tell her.

She lifts her eyebrows.

"But I'll give it a shot," I say.

And then she's gone inside and I'm standing alone beside my truck. I take the time to roll a cigarette, get it lit, and stand there smoking, not even thinking about getting into the cab. I realize that I'm finally beginning to understand what Alice has with Thomas. And why using some love potion would be wrong.

I want to take this slow. I want to savor every moment of it.

But the trouble is, the time's just not there.

Alice

It didn't take long for the desert to work its magic on Alice. It never did. The clamor in her mind had long since gone quiet by the time she'd left the mesquite and creosote bushes of the bajada behind. She was in the foothills of the Rincons now, steadily working her way up a switchback trail, and it was hard to hold on to human concerns under the watchful presence of the uncles and aunts that surrounded her. Palo verde grew here, too, sharing the hillsides with thickets of cholla and the spindly ocotillo that looked like octopi with their heads in the sand, legs sticking up. But the stands of giant saguaro loomed above them all. They were the spiritual guardians of this land and Alice was always at peace among them.

One of her first teachers had been an aunt growing in these very hills, a venerable spirit whose home in this world was a tall, many-armed cactus that appeared in *huya aniya* as an old Native woman, broad-faced and short, with an ever-present smile. Like all the aunts and uncles, she was nameless, but Alice had taken to calling her Aunt Mother, because she had neither, and Aunt Mother imbued the qualities of both for a jackalope with the newfound ability to walk as a five-fingered being, and a hunger to understand the mysteries that underlie the world.

Aunt Mother was already well over two hundred years old when Alice first met her — an impressive age for her host plant, though barely childhood for the wizened spirits that inhabit the creosote which took a hundred and twenty years to grow a single foot in height. But the creosote spirits kept to themselves. Their thoughts went inward and deep into the earth, unlike the friendlier spirits who were more ready to share their knowledge with others.

While it was Aunt Mother who had first steered Alice to her human teachers, the two had maintained a companionable friendship for many years. But then lightning struck Aunt Mother's host plant one night, and the Grace called her back into the heart of Mystery.

Alice still made a point of coming back on a regular basis to where the old saguaro had once stood. She'd sit on a great slab of granite and look out across the foothills. Just below that great flat rock, Aunt Mother lay where she'd fallen decades ago. Her flesh had long since been consumed by insects and all that remained of her great length were her woody ribs and a few old spines and slabs of dried skin that still lay at her base where the lightning had struck. The base itself was barely knee-high to Alice, a few ribs arching out of it like a fountain.

Though she still missed Aunt Mother, this was not an unhappy place for Alice. Here, in *el entre,* between this world and *huya aniya,* the world of the spirits, she felt closer to her old teacher than she did anywhere else. Here, she appeared between her old skin and her new — a human woman with a jackalope's long drooping ears and small antlers pushing up out of her hair. Here, she belonged to neither the past nor the present, to what she had been or what others would have her be.

Here, she belonged only to herself.

So it was here she came today and settled herself on the big smooth rock, her mind at peace as she absorbed the quiet that surrounded her. She might have been here five minutes, she might have been here an hour — time was hard to judge in *el entre* — when a high-pitched *kee-ahrrr* came down from the sky above. She looked up to see that the hawk had followed her and watched as it came gliding down towards her. Just as it reached the ground, it transformed into a small, dark-haired Latina who had to take a few quick steps to keep her balance.

"Hello, Bettina," Alice said.

The other woman turned and smiled. "I don't think I'm ever going to learn how to do that as gracefully as I'd like."

"It could be worse. At least you can fly. I would love to see the world as you can from up high."

Bettina came to sit beside her. "*Sí,* it's an amazing sight."

They had met a few years ago in the spiritworld, when Bettina had been searching for her missing grandmother, and become friends both in that world and this until Bettina left the desert for a time. Upon her return, the two resumed their friendship as though Bettina had never been away.

"Was that you I saw earlier?" Alice asked. "Down by Avenda Javalina?"

Bettina shook her head. "It was probably one of *los peyoteros,* setting out early, or getting home late. You know how they are."

"Yes, it seemed a very male energy."

"Though not so male as your friend, Changing Dog."

"What do you mean?"

Bettina shrugged. "It's all the gossip. Cousins speculating on how it will all turn out. Considering his nature, how he chases after anything in a skirt, it doesn't look good. But for the record, we're most of us rooting for you."

Alice couldn't help herself. "Except for?"

"Well, Ramona for one. But that's more because she doesn't want Corina to win than because of any ill-will she might feel towards either of you."

"Win, lose." Alice frowned. "It's not a game. It's our lives."

"I know. It doesn't seem fair. But then life itself isn't fair and for most of us, the rules aren't so specific and clear."

"You won't hear me thanking Corina."

Bettina see-sawed a flat palm in the air between them.

"Except without her," she said, "you would never have known this shape you wear today. And all your studies, *la medicina,* the learning..."

"They are my doing," Alice said firmly. "Not hers. Yes, she allowed me to walk on two legs as a five-fingered being, but whatever else I have achieved, I've done it on my own, or with the help of my teachers."

"*Sí,* más o menos."

"More or less what?"

Bettina gave another shrug. "Perhaps that was Corina's hope in the first place. That you would take her gift and gain a larger spirit through it."

"Ah."

"I know," Bettina said. "It's difficult to be grateful for what seems like a backhanded gift."

Alice took a long breath. She was aware of her body, this place, her connection to Bettina and everything around them.

"No," she said. "It's not such a backhanded gift."

"Except that Changing Dog won't live up to his name."

"I can't really blame him for that," Alice said. "I can't even blame him for not finding love the way I have with Thomas. We can't choose who we will love — or who will return our love."

But as she spoke, she remembered that night almost a hundred years ago, when Corina had told the two new changed beings who stood before her to help each other. Changing Dog hadn't helped her so much. But how much had she helped him?

"You always make me think," she told Bettina.

Bettina laughed. "Oh, yes. I am so very wise."

"No, it's true."

"So what have I made you think of today?"

"That I haven't helped Changing Dog any more than he's helped me." She sighed. "He keeps saying that he and I should be together."

Bettina put a hand to her mouth to hide a smile.

"Have you ever slept with him?" she asked.

Alice shook her head. "I'm probably one of the few women in this area, cousin or human, who can say that."

"Oh, he's not so bad."

"But close." Alice regarded the other woman for a moment. "Don't tell me you have."

"No, no. But he's a...I was going to say handsome man, but it's not that. You feel his presence in here." She laid a hand between her breasts. "And then there is that promise in his eyes."

Alice shrugged.

"And were you never tempted?" Bettina asked.

"No. I have my Thomas. What about you?"

"I have *mi lobo*."

That made Alice smile. "How is that wolf of yours?"

"I don't know. I'm flying north today to find out."

Alice could never stop the small twinge of jealousy that arose whenever she thought of couples such as Bettina and her wolf. Because of their nature, they would be very long-lived and have many more years to share with each other than humans might. If only it could be the same for her and Thomas. But Thomas was wholly human, and like a human, he aged where she remained unchanged by the years. His growing old didn't alter how she felt for him. It only troubled her because it would make their time together shorter than it otherwise could be.

She had tried bringing Thomas into the spiritworld — time spent there by humans increased their longevity — but it was the one part of her life that he didn't want to share.

"I don't want to be changed like that," he told her. "I was born human; I plan to die the same way."

"Even if it's sooner than you have to?"

He shrugged. "We each have the years allotted to us. Who am I to mess with that?"

"You took up exercising," Alice said. "For your health. Because it would prolong your life. How is this different?"

"I don't know," Thomas said. "It just is."

It was so frustrating.

"I can't imagine you as a couple," Bettina said.

Lost in her thoughts of Thomas, Alice gave her friend a puzzled look.

"I mean you and Jim," Bettina added.

Alice shifted mental gears. Of course Bettina hadn't been referring to Thomas.

"Oh, I know," Alice said. "I can't imagine it either. But perhaps he can. Perhaps he keeps repeating it, not for convenience's sake, but because he is sincere."

Bettina gave her a searching look. "So you would —"

"No, no. There's no one for me but Thomas."

"Then what are you saying?"

Alice shrugged. "He came to me today looking for a love potion which I refused to make for him."

"You did right," Bettina said.

"Yes, but that doesn't mean I couldn't help him in some other way."

"How could you help such a free spirit to settle down? Is it even possible that he could?"

"I don't know," Alice said.

But by the time she'd said good-bye to Bettina and was on her way back home, she knew that she had to try.

Bess

Laurel tried to get a rise out of me when I got back to our room, but I wouldn't bite. Instead I sat on the bed with my arms around my drawn-up knees and rested my head against the backboard. I know I had a silly grin on my face, but I didn't care. I also had a stirring deep inside — the itch that can't not be scratched, as our sister Adie would say.

Laurel went over to the window and looked down on the parking lot outside the café.

"He's still there," she said.

"What's he doing?"

She shrugged. "Nothing much. Just leaning against the side of his truck, smoking a cigarette." She turned to look at me, laughter in her eyes. "And he's got that same silly grin you're wearing."

"Really?"

"Really." She looked out the window again. "Maybe I should go check out that dance club downstairs and leave you the room."

"Oh, no," I said. "It's too soon to have sex."

Laurel's eyebrows rose. "Since when?"

"I mean it's too soon for someone you're going to be spending a few days with."

"And I repeat, since when? If you're only going to have a few days together, I say make the most of them."

I got up from the bed and stood beside her. "He does look awfully good, standing down there."

"All alone. Bulge in his pants."

I gave her a whack on the arm, but I have to admit I did look. He was too far away to tell.

"Maybe he's got a friend for you," I said.

"Yeah, probably a girlfriend."

"Will you stop already?"

"I will," Laurel said. "I promise. Just as soon as someone male makes a pass at me. That's all I ask. He doesn't even have to be cute. He just has to be a he."

I couldn't help it. I started to laugh.

"What's so funny?"

It took me a moment to get the words out.

"Be a he," I finally managed. "It just sounds funny."

And for no reason, that set me off again. Laurel tried to look put out, but I could see her lips twitching, laughter bubbling in her eyes. Then she started to laugh, too. We stood there at the window, leaning against each, trying to catch our breath. It took the sound of Jim's truck starting up before we could stop.

"Well, there goes your chance for a night of pleasure," Laurel said as we watched the pickup pull out of the parking lot.

"What makes you think a night in my sister's company isn't pleasurable?"

Laurel poked me with a stiff finger. "Don't you start."

"Oh, for god's sake."

"I'm kidding," Laurel told me and went to sit on the bed.

We say that a lot.

I joined her on the bed, the two of us sitting up against the headboard. I don't know how many times we've done exactly this, just hanging out together. Even before we started touring we'd escape to our bedroom at all times of the day or night, sometimes sharing intimacies, sometimes just being together.

"You know," Laurel said after awhile, "a funny thing happened to me out in the desert. I think I finally started to understand how Elsie can spend all the time she does in the woods back home."

Our sister Elsie could spend a whole afternoon sitting in one spot, looking at a mushroom, or sketching some bug, and we never could understand the attraction. It wasn't that we didn't like the hills and fields; we could be as much the tomboy as Sarah Jane or the younger twins. We just couldn't get into the detail of it the way that Elsie would.

But Laurel was right. The hike we'd gone on today had really opened my eyes, too. I couldn't remember one moment of being bored or wanting to be somewhere else. It was more, "One afternoon isn't long enough. I want to spend however long it takes for me to absorb everything I can." It wasn't something I'd ever experienced before.

"Do you know what I mean?" Laurel asked.

I nodded. "It did feel special — and not because of Jim being there," I added at Laurel's smirk. "There was this whole connected thing happening. Like I really felt in tune with every little thing around us."

Laurel forgot about teasing me. "That's exactly what I mean. It was so different from the way we connect through music."

"Well, music connects us with people instead of a landscape..."

"And that's great," Laurel said. "Except when they go weird on you."

I smiled. Although we only had the one CD, we already had people who would email us or come to the gigs and tell us about how we'd changed their lives. Some of them were sincere, and it meant a lot coming from them. But some of them were just sucking up — you could always tell the difference.

We loved playing on stage, but the thing we liked best was when we got to play with other musicians and that inexplicable frisson comes whispering up your spine because the music is just right. I think the best music happens on porches and in kitchens, or afterhours in clubs and off the stage at the folk festivals. You're no longer performing. Instead you fall into the music and some kind of magic happens that embraces everything, even the odd bum note you might play.

"I wonder if Jim knows any of the local musicians," I said. "Because it would be so cool to play with people that have their roots in the land here."

"Better yet," Laurel said, "would be to play with them out in the desert. Up on some high mountaintop like where we were today."

I closed my eyes, imagining it, then started when Laurel gave me a nudge.

"What?" I said.

"You been sleeping for about half an hour," she told me.

"I haven't."

"You have."

She pointed at the clock and I saw she was right.

"You should just get undressed and go to bed," she said.

So I did.

Ramona

The coyote came out of a dry wash and trotted to the rise where Ramona was sitting, watching the house that Thomas Young shared with Alice Corn Hair. Ramona smiled but she didn't look around.

"I know what you're doing," Corina said.

A woman stood where the coyote had been, dressed all in black with her silver and turquoise jewelry winking in the starlight.

"I'm not doing anything," Ramona said. "I'm just enjoying the night."

"Do you think it's fair to play with people's lives like this, just to settle a grudge?"

"I don't play with people's lives. You do."

Corina shook her head. "No, what I do is give them a chance to enrich their lives. The choice as to whether or not they take it is theirs."

"There's no choice involved," Ramona said. "Who'd hold on to living half a life when they find out they can have a complete one?"

"You know I'm sorry about what happened with William."

"Yeah, you keep saying that."

"And you would have left him anyway."

Ramona nodded. "Probably. But you should have left it up to Billy and me how that'd all work out."

"So he shouldn't have had a chance to have more? He should only have had what you could give him, for as long as you felt like giving it to him?"

Ramona turned to her. "You didn't see the look on his face when he recognized the rattlesnake in me."

"I had no idea that would happen," Corina said. "Honestly. I didn't even know you were seeing him, and I had no idea he had such a phobia about snakes."

Ramona shrugged. "It's old history. We're working on a new story now."

"But it's not your story," Corina said. "It's Changing Dog's. And Corn Hair's."

"And yours."

Corina hesitated, then nodded. "And mine."

"So all I'm doing is writing in a new character," Ramona said. "A wild card — just to keep things interesting." She settled her unblinking gaze on Corina's. "Don't you like it when things are interesting?"

"Not when people get hurt."

"People always get hurt," Ramona said.

She turned her attention back to the house. There were no lights on, but she knew the occupants weren't sleeping.

"It's just part of living," she added.

But Corina was already gone.

"Do you want a piece of advice?" a new voice asked.

Ramona looked over to where one of the uncles was watching her from a nearby saguaro. Only his face was visible from the accordion-like bellows of his skin.

"Not particularly," she told him, "but why am I sure that won't stop you?"

"Whenever you interfere in another's life," the uncle said, "that disruption will come back to you."

"Corina's life is one big interference."

"Perhaps. But she does nothing for herself. It is always done for others."

"Yeah, she's such a saint," Ramona said. "And I suppose that makes all her screw-ups okay."

"Everything we do comes back to us," the uncle said. "Don't think that Corina is unaffected by what she does."

"So tell me, just *how* she is affected?"

The uncle slowly shook his head. "You must ask her that yourself." He paused a moment, then added, "Or you could ask Rosa."

Ramona suppressed a shiver and managed to give the uncle a nonchalant wave of her hand.

"Oh, there's no need to involve her," she said.

The uncle smiled. "There's nothing happens in the desert that doesn't involve her. Surely your parents and teachers told you that?"

Ramona didn't know her parents and had yet to meet a being she respected enough to allow them to teach her anything. She looked around herself. For a long moment, every shadow seemed to hold its breath. The sky itself appeared to be watching her.

"No," she said, her voice uncharacteristically subdued. "No one ever told me that."

The uncle gave her another smile. "Don't look so worried. Arguing with Corina isn't likely to attract her attention."

"Of course," Ramona said.

She stood up and brushed the dirt and dust from her legs. Turning to the saguaro, she gave him a respectful nod of her head.

"Thanks for the conversation," she said.

Then she headed off through the creosote and cacti at a quick walk. Behind her, the saguaro uncle's neighbor chuckled.

"Perhaps there's hope for that one yet," the uncle said.

"Yes," his neighbor said. "And when her time is done, Rosa will undoubtedly see that she is reborn as one of us."

The uncle chose to ignore the sarcasm.

"Where there are shadows," he said, "there must be a light to cast them."

"I agree," the neighbor said. "But the light doesn't burn in her. It's only fear that makes her respectful and cautious. And that will wear off as soon as she puts some distance between herself and your conversation with her."

Bess

"Seriously," Laurel said.

We were in the Cup Café with Jim for breakfast the next morning, the two of us sitting across the table from him, a scatter of coffee mugs and the remains of our breakfast dishes between us. With her weight on her elbows, Laurel leaned closer to Jim.

"What tribe are you from?" she asked.

Jim glanced at me and smiled.

"Like I told Bess," he said. "I'm not an Indian. I just have that look."

"It's a good look," Laurel said, leaning back in her chair. "And nothing to be ashamed of. We're not like some people you might have run across before. We've dated Kickaha boys from the rez back home."

"Though not at the moment," I said, then realized that might have come out wrong. "I mean, we're not dating *anyone* at the moment."

Okay, that was worse, but it was too late to take it back.

"We just think it's kind of cool," Laurel said, taking up the conversation before I could say something even dumber. "Having your roots go back as far as they do — way back before *our* ancestors showed up here and took it all away from your people."

Jim shook his head. "I'm not embarrassed. And if you're talking ancestry, my people were here before the Indians, so they've got whole other issues."

"What do you mean before the Indians?"

I was afraid that he'd think we were giving him the third degree, the way Laurel was going on, but I had to admit that the whole thing had me curious, too.

Jim shrugged. "My people are the ones that didn't make it into the history books."

"And?" I asked when he didn't go on.

"And nothing. Nothing much, anyway. They were here and they got pushed out of their lands by the Indians the same way the Indians got pushed out by the Europeans."

"But what were they like?"

"I don't know. Like me, I guess."

"Are you playing the mysterious card?" Laurel asked. "Because I have to tell you, it's working. I haven't a clue what you're talking about, but I do want to know more." She looked at me. "Do you know what he's talking about?"

I shook my head.

When we turned back to Jim we found him studying us with an odd expression. I realized after a moment that he was trying to decide whether or not to tell us more. That made me even more curious.

"Let me show you something," Jim said.

"Will we need hiking boots to see it?" Laurel asked.

He laughed. "No, it's just across the street."

"Too bad. I enjoyed yesterday afternoon."

"We can go out again later today," he said. "I thought you might still be tired from yesterday's hike."

"No way," we said at the same time.

Laurel and I turned and laughed at each other.

Jim smiled. "Then we'll do it. But first I'd like you to see this."

He dropped a few bills on the table to cover the cost of breakfast. When he got up, we followed him outside. It was just going on to eleven and though it was only March 22nd, it was already Tyson County summer hot outside, but without the humidity.

"You should visit in the summer," Jim said when I mentioned it. "It gets up into the hundreds every day."

"But it's a dry heat, right?" Laurel said.

"Yeah. And we have dry rain, too."

"What?"

"Local joke for the *touristas,*" he explained.

He led us through the parking lot and across Toole Avenue to what looked like a large refurbished warehouse or factory. Jim explained how it now housed artists' studios and the Museum of Contemporary Art in Tucson, which was where he was taking us. My heart kind of sank as we stepped into the gallery. It was like some of the ones in Newford that our sister Elsie's taken us into where there's usually just a few paintings hanging in some immense, otherwise empty space and the paintings look like they've got more in common with design than what I think of as art.

The show on exhibit here was just a bunch of large canvases with various, perfectly-made circles of different colors set in neat rows, filling each canvas. It reminded me of a tongue-in-cheek quick history of art I'd overheard on a break during one of our gigs back east: Used to be people couldn't draw very well, then they could, and now they can't again.

"I'm out in the desert a lot," Jim said as we walked through the gallery. "Day and night."

"After yesterday," I said, "I can see why."

He nodded. "There are a lot of us desert rats living here in Tucson. And we go out for any number of reasons."

He stopped at a desk and the young woman sitting behind it looked up from her computer screen, smiling when he asked her to turn on the music and lights downstairs.

"That's where I first met Stu," he went on. "In the desert. I kept running into him late at night with that big camera of his, taking pictures by moonlight and starlight and sometimes it seems like no light at all."

"There you go," the woman said as she returned to her desk. "There should be some flashlights at the bottom of the stairs."

"Thanks," Jim said.

"Flashlights?" Laurel asked.

"Patience," Jim told her.

The artist was Stu Jenks and the exhibit was called "The Open Circle Cairn Project." It was an installation, but nothing like the lame ones Elsie's taken us to in the past. Each step we took down the wooden stairs to the basement where the exhibit hung reminded me of nothing so much as that time back in Tyson County when Laurel and I were kidnapped by fairies. You didn't know? It's a long story, and it's why we ask that question about whether or not people believe in fairy tales, but I don't have room to tell it here. Right now all you need to know is that, like that Monty Python character who claimed he'd gotten turned into a newt, we got better. Or rather we got back.

But fairyland wasn't something you ever forgot — even if you wanted to, which I sometimes did. It changed you, and that's what this felt like, but in a better way than being kidnapped by fairies did.

Like we were moving from one world into another.

Being changed.

Here's what the place was like: Imagine an enormous basement, completely dark except for a faint circular illumination emanating from the floor at the far end. The air was cool, almost chilly, and soft, low-key instrumental music drifted from hidden speakers. Large wooden support beams were scattered throughout and, far down the room by the light, ethereal photographs hung on the walls, almost invisible.

Jim handed us each a tiny flashlight from a basket at the bottom of the stairs. As we walked the length of the room to where the photographs hung, we could see that white mini-lights defined a large, open-ended circle formed by a foot-wide trough cut deeply into the cement floor. Sweet-smelling hay, into which the strings of lights were set, marked the edge. Except Jim explained that the trough was an optical illusion. It wasn't really there. And here's a weird thing: even when we came right up to it and we knew that it was merely a trick of the light, it didn't change our initial impression.

The illusion felt stronger than what was actually there, creating a welcoming space that felt larger than it was and seemed to lay outside of time. We entered the open end of the circle and did a slow turn, feeling the magic and mystery of the place.

When we finally left the circle, I turned my attention to the photographs and realized that this was part of Jenks's wonderful gift: the ability to create truth out of illusion.

The photographs were small and we had to use the flashlights to see them clearly. They were mostly desert night scenes — cacti and rock formations — to which Jenks had added fiery spirals and circles of light.

"Does he Photoshop the designs?" Laurel asked.

Jim shook his head. "He uses a Zippo lighter."

To me, it didn't matter how he did it. They were just magic. In that basement, in the sweet-smelling coolness, viewing each print with key chain flashlights...the photographs became windows into another world, where natural scenes of desert landscapes revealed their spiraling energies to us — not simply as static images, but with ghosts of motion.

We'd gone down to the basement giggling a little at the dark and the mysterious lights and the whole sweet *oddness* of the presentation. As the cool air touched our skins, as our eyes adjusted to the dimness and the darkness gave up some of its shadows, as we stood before the photographs, playing the beam of a flashlight upon them or squinting in the half-light, as we stepped again into the straw circle and the outer world fell away, our voices grew hushed and we fell silent. I can't say where the others went, but I felt literally transported to some other place where I drank deeply of a peace that was at once bright and shadowed and bittersweet.

I don't know how long we were down there, looking at the pictures, sitting in the middle of the straw circle, listening to the music. I just know that time passed at its own pace and we were all reluctant to leave. But eventually, we emerged back into the gallery upstairs once more. And then we were outside, blinking in the sunlight.

"That was amazing," I said.

Laurel nodded. "Except..." She turned to Jim. "I don't see how it explains your ancestors."

"I suppose it doesn't," he said.

"Then why did you want to show us the exhibit?"

"Not that we're complaining," I added.

Laurel shook her head. "Not at all. It's just..."

"When you were down in the exhibit," Jim said, "did you feel like you needed to understand it, or was it enough just to experience it?"

"Mostly just being there," Laurel said.

"I guess what I was trying to say is that maybe every question doesn't need an answer. That some things are just always going to be mysteries."

"Like your ancestors."

He nodded. "I mean, I can't really explain them. The Jenks exhibit just seemed like a good way to say that without seeming evasive or rude."

Laurel and I looked at each other, then back at him.

"Works for me," she said.

Alice

Alice went into the desert again on Friday morning, but this time she was out there on her own. Walking. Thinking.

Last night she hadn't been able to decide how she might be able to help Jim. The more she worried at the problem, the further away any solutions seemed to drift. It was like trying to get a clear view of some hidden thing seen through far too many layers of gauze — each time you moved one layer away, a half dozen others fell down to take its place. But today, as she walked up from the lower desert into the foothills of the Rincons, she realized that she might be coming at the problem from the wrong direction.

She knew Jim. Knew him too well, if the truth was told. But she knew nothing of this new woman in his life.

S S S

Thomas was painting when she got back to the house, or at least he was in his studio with the door closed. She hesitated a moment, then went into her own study and phoned the Hole to see who'd been playing there the other night. Once she had their name, she did a search for the group on the Internet and wasn't surprised when the home page for the Dillard Sisters came up on her computer screen. These days everyone seemed to have a Web site.

She looked at their picture and smiled. Bess and Laurel. They were identical twins, pretty and young. But then Changing Dog, for all his years, was young, too. Like Alice herself, he always appeared to be in his late twenties, but unlike her, and for all the promise in his name, he remained virtually unchanged from the rambunctious red dog that had first chased her through the desert night all those years ago.

She wondered which of the sisters had captured his heart.

Checking their itinerary, she saw that the twins didn't have another gig until Saturday night, up in Prescott. Were they still in town, or had they already started the drive up north? If they were in town, maybe she could find out where they were staying, though how likely was it that anyone at the bar would tell her? Performers expected their privacy and she couldn't imagine that any venue would simply give the name of the hotel where they were staying to the first person who happened to call up. But it wouldn't hurt to try.

She picked up the phone, but before she could dial, she heard Thomas come into the room behind her. She swiveled her chair to find him regarding her with an odd expression on his face. She'd noticed him acting a little preoccupied lately, but she'd simply put it down to the way he sometimes got in the middle of a project. Now she realized that there might be more to it than that.

"We need to talk," Thomas said.

She cradled the phone receiver. "What's the matter, Thomas?"

"Us," he said.

She looked at him in surprise. That he felt there was any kind of trouble between them was the very last thing she expected.

She rose from her chair and crossed the room, wrapping her arms around him.

"I love you," she said. "And you're too old to be going through a midlife crisis." She tilted her head back to look him in the eye. "Aren't you?"

He shook his head. "It just feels like you're...leaving."

"Well, I might need to go to Prescott on Saturday night," she began.

But then she understood that wasn't what he was talking about and the realization of what he'd been feeling hit her like a punch in the stomach. How could she have been such a fool? Here she'd been, walking around saying good-bye to all the things in her life for days now. How could he *not* pick up on it? Of course he'd think there was something wrong between them.

"Oh, Thomas," she said. "It's nothing like that."

She took him by the hand and led him to the old leather sofa set in front of the study's picture window. Sitting there, they could look out at their front garden: an organized jungle of barrel cacti, prickly pear, creosote, mesquite, and one old aunt of a saguaro.

"So you're not leaving?" Thomas asked.

"I'm not leaving you...only..."

She hesitated, looking for the words she needed to explain this properly and not finding any of them.

"But?"

"I might be taken away."

"I don't understand."

"Remember when you proposed to me?" she asked. "I told you about it then. About the curse that Jim and I share."

Thomas gave a slow nod.

"Well, the hundred years are almost up."

"That wasn't just a story?"

"Everything's a story," Alice said, unable to keep the hint of a smile from her lips. "But that one was true as well."

"I know. You said that. But it seemed..."

"Too much to believe?"

He shrugged. "I thought it was an...analogy. A way of sharing something that...I don't know. You found too difficult to talk about otherwise."

"Even after you've seen me step into *el entre* and change?"

"I often wonder about that," Thomas said. "How much of it is real — how much I can really see — and how much is simply suggestion that my own imagination has filled in."

"I never told you about my jackalope blood," Alice said. "Or described what I looked like when I'm partly in my other skin. You found that out on your own."

"I'm not always so sure..."

"You've got a painting in your studio that says differently."

She ran her hand along the sides of her head and knew that, for a moment, he could see the jackalope's long ears and the small antlers pushing up out of her brow.

"I'm not saying I don't believe," he said. "I'll believe anything you tell me."

"Then what is it?"

"We don't feel close anymore. There seems to be a distance between us, and it's been growing wider every day."

Alice nodded. "I see that now. And it's my fault. With time running out the way it is for me...for us..."

She let her voice trail off and they sat there quietly for a time, watching the quail and doves foraging for seeds under the bird feeder.

"You know I'll never stop loving you," Thomas said after awhile. "It doesn't matter what you look like."

"I know," she said. "But if Corina takes away my ability to wear a human shape, you'll be living with a jackalope — not a woman."

"It won't matter to me."

"Of course it will matter. We won't be able to cuddle, or make love. We won't be able to take in a show, or go for walks together, or sit out by the pool with a drink to watch the sunset. We won't be able to do anything that couples do. No," she said as he started to shake his head. "Maybe we'll still be able to talk, but everything else will be gone. I'll be a furred cousin living in the house of a five-fingered being, and that just means I'd be a pet. I won't be anybody's pet, Thomas. Not even yours."

"But..." She watched him deflate. "What can we do?"

"Make sure that Jim has someone in his life who cares as much about him as you do for me."

"In two weeks."

"A little less."

He shook his head. "What woman would put up with him?"

"He could change," Alice said. "He'll have to change."

Thomas looked as doubtful as Alice felt.

"So why do you need to go to Prescott?" he asked.

"To see if I can help Jim get together with this girl he's found."

Thomas turned to look at the computer screen that was still filled with the picture of the Dillard sisters.

"Is she one of those two girls?"

Alice nodded.

"They seem like children."

"That's what I thought, too," she said. "But I'm sure they're in their twenties and Jim's as young inside as he looks on the outside, if you know what I mean." She smiled. "Besides, it's not like an age difference ever meant anything where we were concerned."

Thomas returned her smile.

"I have to do something," Alice went on. "If Jim can find someone to care for him the way you do for me by the time we have to meet Corina, she'll let us stay the way we are."

"But he's never listened to you before."

Alice smiled. "I know. So this time I thought I'd try talking to the girl instead."

"What would you tell her?"

"I don't know. I'm hoping for inspiration." She looked at him. "You could come with me."

Thomas shook his head. "I don't think her talking to some old man is going to help matters much. She'll be much more likely to listen to you."

Alice sighed. She wasn't sure anybody talking to the girl would help. Love was a wild thing that came and went of its own volition. You could no more make someone care for a person than you could get them to stop.

"I have to do something," she said.

"Of course you do." He gave her hand a squeeze. "And don't worry. You'll know what to say when the time comes. You always know the right thing to do or say."

Alice didn't have his confidence, but she gave him a slow nod.

ς ς ς

Later, after trying unsuccessfully to get the name of the twins' hotel from the bartender at the Hole, she found herself packing their Subaru Forester. There wasn't much to bring. A small bag of clothes, and then the usual provisions she always took, just in case: water, a bedroll, and some camping gear.

"I'm coming right back," she told Thomas when she had the car packed.

They stood by the side of the house, watching the sun set behind the Tucsons. She leaned against him, enjoying the feel of his arm when he held her. She never tired of the comfortable fit of their bodies, one against the other.

"I don't want to go," she said. "We might have so little time left and I feel I should spend whatever there is with you."

"Whatever time we have, we'll make the most of it," he said. "But you'll figure this out. You always do."

She smiled. She was glad that they'd talked. He was his old self again — strong and assured. So much so that she was ready to forget the trip. But that would solve nothing.

She tilted her head and they kissed.

"Until Sunday," she said.

Bess

Jim took us to a place called Sabino Canyon in the afternoon. It was way more touristy than yesterday's hike, but he wanted us to see the different landscape in these mountains, the Santa Catalinas on the north side of the city, and especially in this canyon. So after parking in a crowded parking lot and bypassing the T-shirt vendors and gift shop, we walked up a steep, narrow paved road with dozens of other people, moving to the side whenever one of these little trams went by taking the folks too lazy, or unable, to hike.

The Santa Catalinas seemed more lush than yesterday's Tucsons — at least they did here in the canyon along Sabino Creek. Tall grasses thrived on the banks with cottonwoods and sycamores rising up above them — large trees, not the little palo verde and mesquite that we'd seen out in the desert. It was green, green, green. But as the road criss-crossed the creek, you'd get wonderful views of the canyon sides with stands of saguaro climbing up to the ridges, and there were still cacti growing among the more familiar vegetation.

I went down to the creek at one point to touch the trees. I loved the sycamores with their smooth, mottled bark.

Jim smiled when I mentioned how much I liked them.

"Those are Alice's trees," he said.

"Who's Alice?"

"She's kind of a cousin. We've known each other forever. She lives near the Rincons —" He pointed south and east. " — with her husband Thomas. That's Thomas Young, the artist."

"Never heard of him," Laurel said.

"Our sister Elsie's the art expert in our family," I explained.

Laurel nodded. "But ask us about music, and we're your gals."

"He's a well-known Southwestern artist," Jim said, "specializing in desert landscapes."

I'd seen a million of them already in every gallery window that we'd walked by in town and had stopped paying attention to them pretty quickly. I liked the real thing way better.

"Why are they your cousin Alice's trees?" I asked Jim.

He shrugged. "Everybody's got spirit connections — you know, animals and plants and places they connect to."

"You mean like totems?"

"Maybe. I don't know. I always got the sense that totems were kind of preordained by your genetics, or the spirits themselves. The way Alice connects to the sycamores is more personal. It's like the first time she saw them, she immediately recognized an affinity to them. When she's among them, she feels..." He gave another shrug. "Heartened."

"So what are your spirit connections?" Laurel asked.

"The senita," he said without even having to think about it.

I liked that there was no hesitation. Maybe he was vague about his ancestors, but at least he was willing to share what touched him personally. I thought that was more important anyway.

"What's that?" I asked.

"They're like the organ pipe cacti, but not as tall — say, ten feet, tops. Their range is more down in Mexico, but you can find some of the hardier ones growing in Organ Pipe Cactus National Monument. That's south of where we were hiking yesterday."

"What is it that draws you to them?"

He shrugged. "I don't know. I just like their company. They're old spirits, but they're friendlier than the creosote who, next to Rosa, are the oldest."

"Rosa?"

"She's one of the first people — she showed up when Raven was putting the world together in the long ago. They say all the cacti spirits came from her."

"When you say spirits," Laurel said, "are you talking about actual, step-up-and-shake-your-hands spirits?"

I knew exactly what she was getting at. The fairies that had kidnapped us back home in hill country had been the spirits of 'sang — what other folks call ginseng — so you can see how we'd be rightfully nervous about any kind of fairy spirit. Or at least I was. Sometimes I thought Laurel would like nothing better than to meet up with them again. Not in a kidnapping sense, but in a getting-to-know-each-other kind of sense.

"Well, not everybody can see them," Jim said after a moment's hesitation. He paused again, then added, "Does the idea of them bother you?"

Laurel shook her head. "Not really."

"That's not true," I said. "How keen would they be on trying to grab us and then lock us up in some underground hole?"

He gave me a puzzled look.

"I don't see that happening," he said.

"Then it's okay."

Jim looked from Laurel to me.

"Is it just me," he asked, "or is this a strange kind of a conversation to be having on such a nice sunny day?"

"I don't know," Laurel said. "I guess it depends on whether or not you think fairies are strange."

"'Do you believe in fairy tales?'" Jim said.

We both nodded.

"No," he said. "I wasn't asking the question. I was just repeating what Bess asked me back at the Hole the other night. It was one of the first things that came up in our conversation. And now I'm beginning to understand why. And it makes sense that we're all getting along so well."

"And why's that?" Laurel asked.

Jim reached out and lightly pushed a strand of hair away from my face.

"Because like attracts like," he said.

"What about opposites attracting?" Laurel asked.

But I gave her a poke in the ribs and Jim just laughed.

"Come on," he said. "We've got a ways to go still. Unless you'd rather ride in the tram?"

We didn't dignify that with an answer.

⊑ ⊑ ⊑

When we got higher up in the canyon, Jim led us from the blacktop down into the creek bed. Most of it was dry — like all the rivers I'd seen around here so far. That's one of the things I love about driving around Tucson: crossing over "rivers" that are just bands of dry sand cutting through the city.

The creek bed here was much wider than it had been at the bottom of the canyon, with water meandering down from higher up in small streams to form pools large enough to wade in. The large rocks were worn smooth and there were people everywhere, doing pretty much what we were: taking in the sun, eating their lunches, making out. Well, we weren't making out, but that was only because Laurel was here. And we weren't eating, but that was only because Jim hadn't yet unpacked the picnic lunch he'd brought.

He found us a nice sunny rock away from most of the people and we just settled in to enjoy ourselves. It could have been any city park except we were way up in these beautiful mountains, surrounded by desert. We loved it. No pressures, no weird women showing up with nasty agendas. Just good company on a perfect day.

⊑ ⊑ ⊑

And it really was a great day. Jim was so easy to be with. What I especially liked about him was this knack he had of making Laurel feel totally welcome, but making me feel special at the same time.

"You know he could be a keeper," Laurel whispered to me at one point.

I just smiled.

Later, we left the truck in the Hotel Congress parking lot and had dinner that night in a cozy little restaurant on Fourth Avenue called La Indita that Jim told us specialized in Tohono-Tarascan Mexican food. It seemed a lot like Tex-Mex food I've had before except the sauces were way more flavorful and the salsa had a nice bite to it. I loved the little patio out back where we ate, sharing tortilla chips with the sparrows and playing spot-the-lizard on the walls.

As we walked back to the hotel from there, Jim suggested a night drive into the desert. Laurel — bless her soul — begged off, so we saw her to the foyer then got into that old pickup of Jim's and off we went. Finally alone.

From all the driving around we'd been doing, I figured out that we were heading back out through the Gates Pass even before we got there. We'd missed the sunset, so it was dark by the time we got up into the pass. I was surprised at how many lights I saw in the valley beyond. It hadn't seemed nearly so populated, seeing it in the daytime, and I'd been too caught up by the amazing show the sun had put on while it sank to notice after the sunset the other night.

Once we were down in the valley, Jim turned to the left this time. We passed the Old Tucson Studios where they were supposed to have made all kinds of cowboy movies way back when, though it was pretty much just a theme park now. After that we were in the desert, riding the ribbon of blacktop as it led us through the night.

At some point Jim turned off and we rode dirt roads for awhile. Then he finally pulled over and killed the engine. It was so quiet that the ticking of the engine as it cooled down was loud.

"Come on," Jim said.

He grabbed a blanket from the bed of the pickup and led me up a small rise. He shook it out and laid it on a clear bit of ground. When he sat down beside me, he put his arm around me and I snuggled in close. The moon was up and the way its light fell on the hills around us turned the whole desert into a magical dreamland. I half expected these spirits Jim had been telling us about earlier to come stepping out of the saguaro and other cacti.

"This is nice," I said.

"I've got no complaints. Perfect company, perfect setting."

"So where do you live?" I asked.

Jim made a motion with his hand that could have meant anything.

"Out here," he said. "In the desert."

"No, I mean really."

"Really," he said, smiling. He pointed to the truck. "That's my home. I've got a mattress in the back and that's where I sleep except during the rainy seasons. I love falling asleep as I look up at the stars."

"And in the rainy season?"

"I put up a tarp to keep out the wind and rain. It gets cold, but we don't have the kind of weather you'd get."

"It's not uncomfortable?"

He shrugged. "I'm used to it. But it's best on a night like tonight when you're snug under the blankets with the big sky cool and clear above you, the stars looking down."

"I'd like to try it some time," I told him.

Jim didn't say anything for a long moment. I leaned my head on his shoulder and waited.

"Do you have a cell phone?" he asked finally.

I gave a little shake of my head against his shoulder. "Who did you want to call?"

"No one. I just thought you might want to call Laurel, tell her you weren't coming back tonight."

I laughed. "Oh, I think she already knows that."

And that's how I ended up in his bed in the back of his pickup and we finally got to make love.

Ramona

The saguaro spirits had spooked Ramona last night with all their talk of Rosa and repercussions, spooked her enough so that, when she left their stand, she didn't go creeping up on Alice and Thomas's house as she'd first planned. Instead, she abandoned the desert and went back into town, walking up Speedway and stopping at the first roadhouse she came across. A half-dozen pickup trucks and motorcycles were in the parking lot. The sign above the door had a letter burned out so that it simply read "B_R."

"Brrr," Ramona read aloud, holding the "R." She smiled and the uneasiness that had been dogging her lost its hold. "Not in this weather, *amigo*."

But if the evening was still warm, it was air-conditioned inside. There, in the cool, smoky gloom, she kept the tequila shooters coming and danced with whomever could keep up with her. By closing time she'd worn out a half-dozen hopeful men, but the last one had staying power. He was a lanky cowboy, visiting from out of town, and no one had awakened any latent cousin blood in him.

She touched a finger to the tip of his nose and grinned.

"It's your lucky night, cowboy," she said and went back to his motel with him, making a different kind of mischief from the kind that would disrupt any of Corina's plans.

It was almost enough to let her forget about the coyote woman, about Rosa and red dogs, jackalopes and all.

But late in the afternoon she left the cowboy still sleeping in his motel room and walked back down Speedway, cutting across country when she got near Alice's house. She startled rabbits and various quail foraging under the creosote and mesquite, but she wasn't trying to hide her presence — at least not from cousins. Settling in under a palo verde, she found herself a good view of the back of the house, but her attention kept wandering to the saguaro that grew nearby. If the spirits inside the tall cacti were watching her, they weren't being obvious.

She sighed, thinking of what the old uncle had told her last night.

Rosa, Rosa.

The name went shivering through her, but if the mother of the desert was watching her, she wasn't being obvious about it either.

Ramona returned her attention to the house.

Why was she so worried about what that ancient spirit might do? As though Rosa could be everywhere. Like she didn't have a thousand better things to do than check up on one rattlesnake woman who was maybe working up a little harmless mischief.

Well, mostly harmless.

But there were the stories. There were always stories. How many were true was anybody's guess, but she'd heard that even Cody soft-stepped around Rosa — and that was the Cody of old, who backed down from no one, not today's love-struck pup with his magpie girlfriend.

Ramona hadn't been sure what she'd planned to do here — not specifically. The idea was that if she couldn't set the red-haired banjo player against Jim, then maybe she could drive a wedge into the so-perfect relationship that Alice and Thomas shared. It didn't matter which of the two — Jim or Alice — was loveless on the night they had to face Corina. Only that one of them was.

But if she didn't have an exact plan, she knew that she didn't want Rosa watching her.

She couldn't have put in words what it was about Rosa that made her so nervous. She'd never met her. She didn't know anyone who had. She just knew that attracting Rosa's attention was not a good idea.

She sighed and gave the saguaro spirits another quick glance, then shifted to snake form and went sliding through the brush towards the house. There was no one on the back patio, nor in the studio that led off from it. She wasn't rewarded until she came around to the front of the house and discovered Alice and Thomas talking in Alice's office.

This was better than she'd hoped, she realized as she eavesdropped on their conversation. Once she'd heard enough, she retreated back into the desert and curled up on a sunny rock, soaking up the sun while she waited for Alice to leave.

᱑ ᱑ ᱑

She lingered on that rock for another twenty minutes or so after Alice had driven off before she finally shifted into human form once more. Sauntering up to the front door, she leaned on the bell, stepping back when she heard footsteps approaching.

Thomas opened the door and regarded her for a long moment. Ramona stood with one hip thrust out a little, hand on that hip. She smiled as only she could: promising you everything; all you had to do was invite her in.

"Do you know who I am?" she asked.

"Not precisely," he said. "Does it matter?"

"Not if you invite me in."

"Alice isn't here," he told her.

"Maybe I'm not here to see Alice."

He fell silent, studying her.

"Then you're wasting your time," he finally said.

He started to step back inside.

"You don't have to grow old," Ramona said before he could close the door.

Sex wasn't the only promise she had to dangle in front of him. Truth was, she hadn't really expected it to work anyway.

"What's that supposed to mean?" he asked.

Ramona shrugged. "Maybe Alice never told you, but there are ways to prolong your life."

"I know. Spend time in the otherworld."

"But if you know..."

"Why do I let myself grow old?"

Ramona nodded.

"This is who I am," Thomas told her. "Just like having some kind of animal blood in you is who you are. I don't mind growing old. Why should I?"

"Because there's so much else that you've yet to experience. You can't tell me you've done everything you've ever wanted to do."

"I suppose I haven't. But I like who I am. If I cross over to the otherworld, I'll be changed. Sure, I'll live longer, but who will I be?"

"Whoever you are now. You'll just have more years to be who you are."

"And look where that got Alice," he said. "All those years she's lived, growing and making something of herself, and now there's a night coming up where she's going to lose it all, just because this coyote woman decided that her fate's linked to somebody else's. Somebody who, by all accounts, doesn't much give a damn about anything except himself. I prefer to live my life on my own terms — not as part of a bargain with somebody else deciding my choices."

"I wasn't offering you a bargain," Ramona said. "I was just going to show you how you could live longer."

"Out of the goodness of your heart."

"Yes."

"I don't buy it," Thomas told her. "This kind of thing, it always comes with a price. And just becoming somebody I'm not — that's already a higher price than I want to pay."

For a long moment Ramona couldn't speak, for she suddenly realized that she had somehow fallen into playing Corina's game. What had started out as an attempt to drive a wedge between Thomas and Alice — by offering him something Alice hadn't, or couldn't, or wouldn't — had turned into her genuinely arguing the benefits of realizing one's full potential. There wasn't much difference between waking animal blood in a human to offering him a chance at longevity.

And he was right. Either one changed you forever.

"I'm sorry," she began, but he wouldn't let her finish.

"You should try telling the truth for a change," he said before he closed the door in her face.

Ramona frowned, but bit back the sharp retort that was forming on her tongue.

Tell the truth? There was a novel concept. Why hadn't she considered that before? Finding out you were in love with someone not quite human — it wouldn't make any difference to the old painter on the other side of this door.

He already knew what his lover was. But that red-haired girl, so enamored with a handsome, red-haired man?

It could make all the difference to a human girl such as she. And Ramona would be very careful not to wake any of the sleeping cousins in the girl's blood.

Was it the right thing to do?

Ramona had only to remember the look on Billy's face when he realized he'd been sleeping with a rattlesnake woman.

So maybe she'd strayed in the direction of Corina's tendencies. Maybe she understood the why of what Corina was doing a little better. But so what?

That didn't change her need for a payback of some kind for what the coyote had done to Billy — for the way it had made him look at her. Corina should have checked first to see what waking Billy would mean.

But she hadn't.

Was it so wrong to want a little payback?

And this way...well, even Rosa, if she were looking, wouldn't be able to find fault. Because Ramona was just being honest. She would just be telling the truth.

And everybody deserved to know the truth, didn't they?

On the Road Again

Laurel

I WOKE UP alone in our room in the Hotel Congress with a big grin on my face — like I was the one who'd spent the night with a handsome, red-haired man, instead of Bess. Truth was, I actually felt a bit of that languid, after-sex dreaminess when all I'd done after they let me off last night was go to a nearby cyber café to check up on our Web site's message board. Then I came back here to our room where I slept through the night. And maybe I'd had a busy little hand, just before I drifted off last night, but that wasn't the case this morning. No, this was me connecting with Bess.

I guess it's a twin thing. I've talked to other twins and we all seem to share some level of empathic communication with our old womb-mate, as Elmer Fudd might say. Ha ha.

But seriously, while I can't tell you exactly what it's like for other twins, I do know that it's really strong for Bess and me — no matter how far away from each other we might be. Maybe it's because we're best friends as well as twin sisters.

Bess never seems to think about this kind of stuff — she just rolls her eyes whenever I bring it up — but I do. I mean, think about it: for nine months we were floating together in our mom, just the two of us, pretty much as close as anybody's ever going to get. Sharing the same sustenance, all the same stimuli. But then we come out and maybe we look exactly the same, but inside, we're not at all. When people see similarities in the way we act or talk or the things we like, it's because we know each other so well. It's so easy to be attracted to something because your twin is, even if it's something you wouldn't think would interest you at all. We just understand each other better than most people do. But while we're not the same person, not even close, at the same time there's this invisible connection so that we finish each other's sentences and we always know how the other's doing.

At least that's the way it is for us.

So when I woke up, I just *knew* she was happy. And that made me happy. I carried my good mood down to the café with me and not even the slow service could put a dent in it. I was on my third coffee when I sensed Bess getting close. A moment later, Jim's pickup pulled into the parking lot, and there she was, sitting in the middle of the bench seat, right beside him, a big grin on her face.

And Jim wasn't exactly looking all that sad either.

I nursed that last coffee of mine while they had breakfast and then Bess and I went upstairs to pack. When we got up to the room, Bess threw herself on the bed with her arms stretched out on either side. She turned her head to look at me.

"I think I'm in love," she said.

"I know. I'm jealous."

She sat up. "But good jealous, right?"

I gave her a quick nod. "If there's such a thing, I'm definitely feeling happy-for-you jealous, with just a touch of where-can-I-get-me-mine."

It was true. I *was* a little jealous that she'd found this sudden, deep connection with this handsome guy, but not to the point where I wouldn't want her to have it.

I'd always had lots of boyfriends, but never anyone to die for, if you know what I mean. Never one that totally made my heart sing the way Jim seemed to be doing for Bess. I've had boyfriends I liked a lot, and I always had fun when I was with them, because if it stopped being fun, I broke up with them. But I also knew they weren't the one — the long-term one that you might or might not be lucky enough to find as you make your way through the world.

It's not something I decide the moment I meet some guy. I'm more than willing to grow into that kind of relationship. It just hasn't happened yet.

"He's out there somewhere," Bess said.

That wasn't something I necessarily believed, that everyone has a soul mate somewhere out there in the wide world. But I wasn't going to bring Bess down with that.

"And he's probably a she," I joked instead.

Bess laughed, then sat up on the bed.

"We should pack," she said.

"I'm already done," I told her.

So I sat and played a few tunes on my fiddle while she got her own clothes and toiletries stuffed into her suitcase.

⌐ ⌐ ⌐

I guess we got spoiled from the tours Jim took us on around Tucson, because once the I-10 took us out of the city, heading north to Phoenix, the scenery got pretty dull in comparison. I ended up falling asleep and they had to wake me up when we stopped for lunch in Phoenix. But after Phoenix it got a lot prettier and more dramatic, with less desert and more piney woods as we got up into the Bradshaw Mountains on the way to Prescott.

After awhile Bess and I started to sing some of the old mountain songs from back home, teaching Jim the choruses. Turns out he's a natural, with a resonant singing voice, but when Bess said we'd have to get him to sing a couple of songs with us at the gig, he was all, no way, I couldn't do that.

What's with stage-shy people, anyway?

Prescott seemed nice, if a bit touristy in the downtown area, but who am I to throw stones? *I'm* a tourist here, aren't I?, even if we do have a gig.

We came into town off Highway 69 which turned into what looked like the main drag, what with the courthouse and all. Our hotel was on this street, too, but before we got there we passed something called the Elk's Opera House on our right. The marquee read:

Whatever it was, it was happening tonight, which was too bad because we had our gig and this definitely sounded intriguing.

"Do you know anything about that festival?" I asked Jim as we continued down the street.

"Well, Woodland's a local group," he said, "but this festival's a new thing. I guess the World of Froud's another group and —"

"No, he's an artist," Bess said. She turned to me. "Remember that book of squashed fairies that Elsie got the twins?"

I did, except:

"They were pressed fairies," I said.

"Whatever. He's the artist."

"You say twins," Jim began.

"We've got two sets in our family," Bess told him. "There's seven of us in all."

"Wow."

"And Terri Windling?" I asked. "Is she a musician or an artist?"

"An artist," Jim said. "But she also writes books. Her paintings usually feature desert spirits, but whenever there's something to do with fairies around here, the organizers will try to get her involved. Normally, she doesn't, but I guess this time she said yes. Maybe she knows somebody else on the bill." He smiled. "But she'll die to see her name on a marquee like that — she's really a private person."

I had to shake my head. "So do you know *everybody?*"

"No. I've just met her because she's a neighbor of Alice's and I've been to a couple of the sweats at her place."

Bess turned, leaning her arm on Jim's shoulder, and looked out through the back window with me.

"I wish we could go to the festival," I said. "I'd love to know more about the local fairies."

Jim laughed. "Oh, there won't be anything like that. For them, fairyland only exists in the woods and moors of Britain."

"But...we have fairies here, too."

"Yeah, I know. But I guess they're not romantic enough or something."

"We'll just have to make up for the festival's ignoring them," I said. "We'll play some fairy tunes at the gig tonight — the ones we learned from that 'sangman back home. It's not the music of the desert or this high country, but they've got their own high lonesome sound."

"Now that I'd like to hear," Jim said.

"They're good," I said. "But I still wish we could learn more about the local fairies."

"Well, you never know," Jim said. "You're not gone yet."

We both looked at him, me leaning way forward to see around Bess.

"What do you mean?" Bess asked.

I could hear the twinge of nervousness in her voice even if Jim couldn't. He only shrugged, then gave a nod to a building coming up on our right.

"Here's the hotel," he said.

⑤ ⑤ ⑤

The parking lot was around back and lower in elevation than the Hotel St. Michael itself where we had a room booked, so we had to go up a set of concrete stairs and down a little alley to get inside, but it was great once we *were* inside and had our room. I love these old places. This one was built back in 1900, a huge stone building located right on something called Whiskey Row — no need to guess how that got its name, though a lot of the bars that must have been here during the old mining days are boutiques now.

I took the time to wash my face and freshen up my makeup, then left the room to my traveling companions who seemed in dire need of a "nap." I walked around a little when I got outside, but I'm not much of a shopper and finally settled down in the café next door where I worked on our set list for tonight and then flipped through a copy of *People* Magazine that someone had left behind on the table.

I didn't expect to know anybody — we'd never met the people putting on the house concert, though we gave them a call as soon as we got up to our room — so I was surprised when someone asked if she could sit at my table with me. I started to say, sure, except then I recognized her: Jim's old stalker flame that we'd met in the mountains the other day.

"I don't think so," I told her.

"Look," she started. "I know you must think —"

But I didn't give her time to finish. "Do you know how pathetic it is for you to have followed us all the way here?"

She sighed. "Well, I can be pathetic, but not because I'm some stalker. I didn't follow you. I came for the Faerieworld Festival and just happened to see you sitting in here when I was walking by —"

"Right."

" — so thought I'd come in and apologize for my behavior the other day."

"Apologize."

She nods.

"Oh."

Now I felt a bit like a heel.

"My name's Ramona, by the way."

"I know."

"So do you mind if I sit for a moment?"

I moved the magazine aside so that she'd have room to put down her coffee.

"I guess," I said.

"You have every right to be mad at me," Ramona said once she was sitting down. "I don't know what got into me. I'm usually not that mean."

I couldn't help myself. "Usually?"

She shrugged and smiled. "What can I say? I have one of those personalities that just rubs a lot of people the wrong way."

I don't know why, but I found myself relaxing and even sort of liking her. It's a quirk of my personality. I might have a quick temper, but I'm quick to forgive, too. I guess I just like to see the best in people.

"So are you here for the festival, too?" she asked.

I shook my head. "We're playing a house concert here in town."

"You're a musician?"

"We both are — I mean, my sister and me. We're sort of touring around as a duo."

Ramona nodded. "Red Dog always did love music."

"Who's Red Dog?"

"Red Dog, Changing Dog."

"Oh, you mean Jim. Yeah, Bess first met him at a gig we had in Tucson and they seem to be hitting it off pretty good."

"I'm not surprised. He's a great guy."

I nodded, but my curiosity was backtracking to what she'd said a moment ago.

"Why'd you call him Red Dog?" I had to ask.

She shrugged. "Oh, you know. Changing Dog's his proper name, I suppose, but I always think of him as a red dog because that's his original animal shape."

"What are you talking about?"

"I forgot. You're not from around here. Didn't he tell you anything about how he came to be a five-fingered being? A human," she adds at my blank look.

I shook my head, starting to get a bad feeling.

"Everybody knows it around here," she said.

And then she told it to me, a desert fairy tale that most people would have thought was impossible. But I've been to fairyland. I know these things can be all too real.

"Are you saying he's only into Bess because of this curse?" I asked when she was done. "That he's working on making her fall in love with him so that he can stay human?"

"You're taking this awfully well," Ramona said. "Most people would be just shaking their heads at this point."

"Yeah, well, maybe I've had some experience in things that can't be explained except as magic. And you're not answering my question. Is he running some kind of a scam on my sister?"

She shook her head. "Oh, no. Jim's an honorable guy."

"But you said if he doesn't have somebody in love with him within the next couple of weeks, this Coyote Woman's going to turn him back into a dog."

"No, I said he'd be stuck in his dog shape. Right now he can become a dog whenever he wants."

"So my sister's new boyfriend is a...what? A were-dog?"

"More like a shapechanger."

"And if this Coyote Woman does her mojo on him, he won't be able to become human anymore?"

Ramona nodded. "But he'd still never just use somebody."

I might have put up a brave front, but actually, I was still trying to get my head around the idea that the guy up in the hotel room with my sister actually started out his life as a dog. Just because a person has had a weird experience like Bess and I have, doesn't mean this kind of thing still isn't going to come as a surprise. And that's when I realized that, for whatever reasons of her own, Ramona was probably trying to run her own scam on me. Not knowing that I'd already been to fairyland, she'd probably been expecting protestations of disbelief.

I decided to take a run with that. So I leaned back in my chair and gave her my best *Oh, really, who are you trying to kid?* look.

"And I'm supposed to believe all of this?"

She shrugged. "See that woman sitting at that table in the back?"

I turned to look at the blonde. "What about her?"

"That's Alice Corn Hair. You could ask her."

"What's *she* doing here?"

"I don't know. Maybe you should ask her."

"But —"

"Look," Ramona said. "I'm really sorry. I just came in to apologize, not upset you all over again. I thought you *knew* all of this stuff. That Jim or somebody would have told you."

I was back to not trusting her again because I couldn't shake the idea that the whole reason she'd *really* shown up here was to tell me this story of hers about Changing Dog and Corn Hair and some spirit called Coyote Woman. But she returned my suspicious gaze with an innocent one and I didn't know how to call her on it. I didn't know what the point would even be *to* call her on it.

"I should just go," she finally said and stood up.

I didn't bother replying. Instead, I turned again to look at the blonde woman at the back of the café. I didn't wait to see Ramona leave. Pushing back my chair, I got up from my table and headed for where this Alice Corn Hair was sitting.

She seemed a little — I don't know — self-conscious when I stopped by her table and looked down at her. Like I'd caught her with her hand inside the cookie jar.

"So I suppose you're here for the festival, too," I said. "And you just happen to have stopped in here for a coffee."

She blinked, but then shook her head.

"No," she said. "I'm here because I want to talk to you and your sister."

"So talk."

"Won't you at least sit down? My name's Alice, by the way."

I hesitated a moment, then shook the hand she offered and told her my name.

"So why do you want to talk to me?" I asked as I sat down. "Because I was just talking to this Ramona woman and..."

And what? I wasn't sure where to go with this.

Alice nodded. "Ramona," she repeated. "I know her better as Rattlesnake Woman."

"So you're all animal people?"

"Many of us are."

"And you're really a jackalope?"

"I can be." She paused a moment, then added, "You have some deer blood yourself. And a touch of snake."

"Of course I do."

She shrugged. "I only mention it because it's not such a rare occurrence. What's rare is having access to both shapes. And since I can tell by the look on your face that you find the whole business distasteful —"

"I would have said confusing. Maybe a little freaky, but mostly confusing."

"All right. Since you find it confusing and somewhat troubling, I would make a point of steering clear of Coyote Woman yourself."

"How am I even supposed to know what she looks like?"

"Well, Corina usually favors turquoise jewelry and —"

"Did you say Corina?"

Alice nodded.

"God, I've met her. Back in Tucson."

So that explained why Jim had wanted to avoid her. But then a more immediate concern occurred to me.

"Does this mean I'm going to turn into a deer or something?" I asked.

"Did Corina say she was waking your animal blood?"

"No."

"Then you should be fine," Alice said.

I felt anything but fine. Right now some were-dog was with my sister and this rabbit woman was telling me I was part animal myself. But much as I wanted to go running up to the room, I realized it would be smarter to stay and learn as much as I could first.

"So what was it that you came here to tell me?" I asked.

"To be honest," Alice said, "I had no idea what I was going to say. Or that Ramona would be here."

"Is that story she told me true? The one about you and Jim and Corina?"

"Yes. But believe me, I mean no harm to you or your sister. And I doubt Jim does either."

"Maybe. But you've both got everything to lose if someone doesn't fall in love with him pretty damn fast."

She shook her head. "What will be will be. I would never want happiness for myself at the expense of another's chance at the same."

"How very Doris Day."

She gave me a puzzled look.

"You know, 'Que sera, sera.' Sorry. Music reference. It's a bad habit of mine."

"I can't speak for Ramona or Corina, but I promise I bear you no ill will."

"And Jim? Can you promise me he doesn't either?"

She sighed. "I'd like to be able to make that promise — and I certainly believe he doesn't, or I wouldn't be here — but none of us can really know what's inside another's heart or mind. I can tell you this: he seems genuinely smitten by your sister and I know the regret he feels that they might have so little time together is real."

I sighed. I could put Bess in the same boat: totally head-over-heels in love by this point.

"Is he going to tell her?" I asked. "About any of this?"

"I would hope so." She hesitated, then added, "And it would certainly be better if it came from him."

I knew what she was saying. If I went blabbermouth, Bess could easily not give him a chance to explain and then I might have to live the rest of my days as the one who'd stood between her and true happiness. But she was my sister. I couldn't just stand by and do nothing.

"I don't know what to do," I finally said. "Who to trust, what to believe, anything."

"I can see it would be a difficult choice," Alice said. "Whatever course of action you take, you stand the risk of keeping her safe, or breaking her heart."

I gave her a glum nod.

"And this is what you came all the way from Tucson to tell me?" I asked.

"No. I came to meet you and your sister and, if I felt the affection between your sister and Jim was genuine, to see if I might facilitate the growth of their relationship."

"Because of this curse of yours."

Alice nodded. "But *only* if I thought they cared for each other. And normally, I still would have let nature take its course, but time is short."

I don't know why, but I instinctively trusted and liked her. Maybe it was because of the baby rabbits Elsie took care of one summer after their mother was killed by a neighboring dog. Our own dog Root liked to chase animals, but he wasn't a killer. We'd all loved those little bunnies and the truth was, I could see a bit of them in Alice. Weird as it was, occasionally I'd swear there were long drooping rabbit ears hanging in amongst her blonde hair — just a glimpse and they were gone again.

"What would you do?" I asked. "If you were me?"

"Keep my sister safe," she said immediately, then she sighed. "But the only way to be sure of that is get her away from Jim and no matter how you do that, you'll break her heart."

"And that dooms the both of you."

Alice shook her head. "We were born jackalope and red dog. And then we were given a hundred years during which we could wear either shape. That's more than most get — my people or you five-fingered beings."

"Do you have someone who loves you unconditionally?"

Alice smiled. "Oh yes. His name is Thomas and you couldn't find a kinder or gentler man." Her smile broadened. "And he'd hate this conversation."

"He doesn't take compliments well?"

"He doesn't take talking about magic well."

"And yet you're a couple."

Alice nodded. "But my origins are something we rarely discuss."

"That seems sad. I mean, that you can't share that part of yourself with him."

"Everybody has a secret side of themselves — one that belongs only to them. Thomas shares my interest in the medicine ways and my concerns for the environment. I share all my studies with him. We simply don't talk about —"

She reached her hands up and for a moment there really were long rabbit ears held between her fingers — not to mention a pair of small antlers pushing up from the top of her head. She smiled and let the ears fall. They, and the antlers, were gone before the ears could flop against the sides of her head.

I could feel my eyes going wide.

"Okay," I said. "I just thought I saw..."

"You did."

"But how come I can't see them now?"

"I took you into *el entre* for a moment," Alice said. "That's the place between this world and that of the spirits. Things can appear differently there — more true."

I remembered something she'd said earlier.

"So did I look part-deer?" I asked.

Alice shook her head. "First that deer blood needs to be woken. But I would think well before doing that."

"Because it's bad?"

"No, because it will open you up to whole other way of seeing the world, and of being in it. It can be very illuminating, but also scary. And once it's happened, you can't go back."

"I've already been to fairyland, you know," I told her.

Alice raised her eyebrows.

"It's a long story."

"Such encounters usually are."

"I guess," I said. "And it's sure not something that you forget, although we were told that we would."

"I think it depends on how grounded you are in your own skin, or how well you understand the connections between yourself and *this* world. It's the uncertain mind that becomes uncomfortable with new experiences and needs to compartmentalize even what's obviously meant to be a mystery."

She seemed to have an answer for everything. Not a pat answer. And not a condescending one. Just clear and straightforward. As matter-of-fact as though we were talking about makeup or fiddle tunes.

"You remind me of my mother," I found myself saying.

She smiled. "Most people see me as someone much younger."

"Oh, you look young. But you've got the same, I don't know, air of kind competence about you that Mama does."

"I'll take that as a compliment, then."

"I meant it that way."

Alice was quiet for a moment, then she said, "Maybe you should call your mother and ask her what she thinks you should do."

"It's not exactly her field of expertise. The only person who knows a lot about this kind of thing is my sister Sarah Jane, but she doesn't have a phone."

Alice raised an eyebrow.

"Oh, I know. It's weird. She's gone all back to the land and doesn't use any new-fangled inventions."

I didn't think I'd ever used the word "new-fangled" in a sentence before.

"Is that so bad?" Alice asked.

"Well, no. But do you have to give up *everything?*"

"You'd be surprised how the smallest thing can have such large ramifications. Take a cell phone. It's so small and convenient. But it runs on batteries, which aren't biodegradable. It requires broadcast towers, satellites, and all the services and technology necessary to erect and maintain such systems, and every one of those things has an impact on the environment."

"I never thought about it like that." I paused, then added, "Actually, Sarah Jane has a cell phone — Mama made her get one — but she can only use it to call out because there's no reception down at the house. She has to go up on the mountain behind her place to get it to work."

"So there's no one you can ask."

I shook my head, then looked right into her eyes. "Except for you."

"But I'm part of the problem."

"I trust you anyway."

Alice gave a slow nod. "Then I'd recommend we let Jim tell her in his own time."

"And if he doesn't?"

"He will. Jim can be frustrating in more ways than I can count, but he's an honest and honorable man. In a situation like this, we can trust him to do the right thing."

"Ramona said pretty much the same thing."

"Did she? Well, then there's something she and I actually agree on."

I gave a slow nod.

"So," I said. "If you hadn't run into me here, how were you going to approach me?"

"Actually, I wanted to talk to either you or your sister because I didn't know which of you was involved with Jim. And I thought I'd try after the show tonight."

"You're going to this house concert?"

"I have a ticket and everything."

"Do you want to come with us?"

She shook her head. "I'd rather meet you there, where I can just be a part of the crowd."

I got it.

"You want to check out Bess and Jim on the sly," I said.

She laughed. "Oh, I'd never get away with that. Not with Jim. He'll spot me as soon as he comes in the room."

I supposed he would.

"I've got to tell you," I said. "I'm scared. I don't know how any of this is going to turn out. I don't want anybody to be hurt."

Alice nodded. She reached out and took my hand.

"I know," she said. "You should do what the *curanderas* advise: follow your heart. Trust what it tells you."

"The way Bess is doing?"

"It might be a good thing that she is doing — for both her and Jim."

We left it at that.

Ramona

Ramona stepped out of the café onto Whiskey Row. It was late afternoon, closing in on evening, and the sky was still overcast. She tilted her head, nostrils flaring, but she couldn't smell rain. Not soon, at any rate. Her gaze dropped from the clouded sky to linger on the Yavapai County Courthouse rearing up out of the square of lawn across the street, but she didn't really focus on the clean lines of the big stone building. She was still too deep inside her head, pleased with herself for the potential trouble she'd left brewing in the lives of Changing Dog and his new friends.

Who knew telling the truth could be so effective?

Her attention only returned to the courthouse when the building shimmered and then faded away — along with the rest of Prescott. Street, bars, boutiques, café, hotel — all gone. There were only the mountains around her now, draped with their cloaks of pine and looking down on her.

Ramona wasn't alarmed — she realized immediately that someone had pulled her into the otherworld — but she wasn't particularly pleased either. It showed a decided lack of manners and respect. She turned slowly to see who had been so foolish or brave, a sharp retort forming on her lips until she saw who was standing near her.

The stranger was a tall, Rubenesque woman, barefoot, wearing a dress patterned after a Navajo blanket. Her hair was jet black, falling across her ample breasts in two long braids into which were woven tiny rose blossoms. Her face was broad, creased with laugh lines, and her eyes were so dark they seemed all pupil. A nimbus of light clung to her, as though her spirit was so bright it needed to escape through the pores of her coppery skin because her body couldn't contain the radiance.

Though she'd never met the woman before, Ramona immediately knew who this was. It could only be Rosa. The Mother of the Desert.

Ramona's heart sank. Now she was in for it.

Rosa's gaze was fixed on hers and she wore a beatific smile that did nothing to calm the sudden quick rhythm of Ramona's pulse.

Ramona started explaining herself before the other woman could say a word.

"I didn't do anything wrong," she began.

"I know," Rosa said. "In fact, you did good. You brought them understanding."

"I did?"

Rosa made a circular motion with her hand, as though cleaning a pane of glass, and a window into the world they'd left behind appeared in the air. She motioned for Ramona to look. Through the window Rosa had made, Ramona saw the interior of the café, Laurel and Alice sitting at a table, having an animated conversation. Smiling. Happy. How had *that* happened?

"It's too bad this still won't work out," Rosa said.

Ramona turned to look at her. "You know that for a fact?"

Rosa shrugged. "How could it? These girls are too human."

"Thomas is human and he and Alice get along just fine."

"Thomas is an exception."

"And they're not entirely human," Ramona continued, wondering why she even bothered to argue the point, but unable to stop herself.

"I know," Rosa said. "I see the red deer and even some distant ties to you and your kin. But it's thin blood and it's sleeping, so it makes no difference."

"Unless someone wakes it."

Rosa gave her an amused smile. "And you would do this — considering your strong stand on what you consider to be Corina's interfering?"

"That's different."

It wasn't, they both knew. But Ramona wasn't ready to admit as much. At least not out loud.

"Why doesn't Corina have to pay for her interfering?" she asked instead.

"Corina pays," Rosa said, echoing what the old uncle had told Ramona the other night. "Her coin is merely different from what you would consider steep."

"Whatever."

Rosa studied her for a long moment, then said, "This feud you have with Corina — you should let it go."

"Because otherwise you'll do what? Reprimand me?"

She couldn't believe she'd just said that, but Rosa didn't appear to take offense.

"No," Rosa said. "Because it harms the growth of your spirit."

"What if I'm not interested in spiritual growth?"

Rosa shrugged. "Then it won't matter, will it?"

"I don't understand. Are you really the Mother of the Desert?"

"I was here to see it born. Perhaps I planted a seed or two. Perhaps I nourished what might not otherwise have fulfilled its potential."

"So you are, you're just not going to say it. But it means you're like a goddess, or something, right? Everything and everybody's under your control and protection."

Rosa smiled. "Hardly. I can only offer guidance. Like the mother who teaches her children all she can, but at some point she must let them make their own way into the world. The choices they make must be their own."

"But you punish those who don't follow your rules."

"I have no rules, and the guidance I offer is simple: to treat all you meet as you would be treated yourself. Human, animal, spirit, as well as our green brothers and sisters. And as for punishing, you already do that enough to yourselves."

So why's even Cody nervous around you? Ramona wanted to ask, but that, she discovered, wasn't a question she could actually bring herself to ask aloud.

"Why did you come to me?" she asked instead. "Are you really watching everybody?"

"I came because you drew me to you."

"I don't think so."

"Perhaps not intentionally, but you were thinking so hard on me, how could I not hear? And once heard, how could I not come and see what troubled you so? It's true that the cacti are the most dear to me — after all, our kinship is strong — but even they must make their own way through the shadows of this world. I can't be everywhere, for everyone. But when I'm called, I try to come."

But I wasn't calling you, Ramona wanted to say. I was doing just the opposite, hoping to *not* be noticed.

"You should go home," Rosa said. "Go home and find your own story. None of this concerns you."

"And if I don't?"

Rosa regarded her with that dark gaze and said nothing for a long moment. Then she leaned forward and kissed Ramona lightly on the brow.

"I don't foresee a lot of happiness in the coming days," she said, "but I wish it for you nonetheless."

Ramona tried to decide if that was a promise — a threat of how things would go if she continued to meddle — or if it was the future already laid out before her. Rosa's gentle gaze gave nothing away. And then the Mother of the Desert was gone and Ramona stood once more on Whiskey Row with the courthouse across the street, the café at her back.

Maybe she should go home. Back to Tucson, at any rate. Because she had no den, no nest, no cave, no house — nothing.

She had only herself.

That was always the trouble. It was why she was so angry at Corina, even though she knew she wouldn't have stayed with Billy.

She had only herself, and the momentary comfort she could find in another's arms. But it never lasted because...

She had only herself.

She sighed, and turned to look at the café for a long moment. Then she stepped into *el entre* and headed back to Tucson.

Laurel

David and Emma Johnson had a beautiful, big house on the west side of town, the kind of place that you immediately felt comfortable in: hardwood floors with lots of dark wood trim standing out against the stucco walls; Navajo rugs, rustic Mexican furniture, gorgeous sculptures and paintings everywhere. The rec room they had fixed up for the concert was bigger than some of the clubs we've played in and there was obviously more than enough room in the house for us to have taken them up on their offer for lodgings, but I have this thing about staying with strangers. I like meeting new people, I just don't want to live with them right away.

If we can afford it, I much prefer to get a room in some nearby motel or hotel — at least until I get to know the people. But if there's a next time around for us here in Prescott, I'd definitely stay with the Johnsons.

Both David and Emma were perfect hosts and they either had a lot of friends, or they'd done a bang-up job on the advertising, because there must have been over forty people in attendance. We don't often use sound equipment for a house concert, but I'm glad we let them talk us into it for this one. Not to crank it up, but the room was big enough that subtleties would have easily gotten lost without the PA.

I was curious as to what Jim's reaction would be when Alice showed up, but I didn't learn anything. When I saw her come in, I looked to where he was standing at the back of the room. His head went up and he immediately looked in her direction — like they were connected the way Bess and I are — but then he only smiled and nodded hello.

And then it was time for us to play.

I glanced at Bess. Since she was still fine-tuning her banjo, I thanked the audience for coming and introduced us.

"We saw you have a fairy festival in town tonight," I said after the preliminaries.

A big guy sitting near the front snickered.

"You don't believe in fairies?" I asked him.

He looked around, then shrugged.

"Well, come on," he said.

"Oh, I know. People don't like to think about that kind of thing anymore. But we have 'em back in home in Tyson County. In fact, this first batch of tunes we got from a 'sangman we met in the woods up behind our farm — that'd be a spirit of the ginseng. He was a raggedy fellow and you wouldn't think he could bow a single note out of that fiddle of his, what with the twigs and leaves growing right out of it, but he could play, all right."

I could feel Bess looking at me, wondering, what *was* I doing? But this was only partly in reaction to what we'd been talking about earlier — how for some folks fairies only existed in little English woodlands and dells. Mostly I was doing it for Jim's sake, so that he could see that we'd already touched on the strange in our lives. How maybe a red dog who could be a man wasn't such a stretch for us.

I saw that Alice got it. I couldn't read Jim's face — he'd be a tough guy to play poker with. Other people in the audience just kind of smiled and went along with it, even the big guy that had snickered earlier.

"So we don't have names for these tunes," I said, "and nobody else seems to either. We've asked everybody from the old fellows back home to folks we meet at festivals, like Kenny Baker and Mark O'Connor. And we've never heard anybody else play them either. So I guess what I'm saying here is, if you recognize any of them, we'd like to hear from you."

I turned to Bess and she just shook her head. She toed the set list I'd made up in the café.

"'Tunes in G,'" she read from the list. "Now I get it. Are they the jigs or the reels?"

"Four-four," I told her and she started in on the banjo, setting a pace until I came in on the melody with my fiddle.

We really did get these tunes from a fairy 'sangman — heard him playing them right before he kidnapped us and stuck us in a hole in the ground until our sister Sarah Jane rescued us — and they've always stuck in my head. And they're really not like anything I ever heard anywhere else. I mean, they're recognizably reels, but the timing's a little strange and while for whole bars they'll sound like something any of the old fiddlers we know would play, all of a sudden they'll jump off and go someplace strange. Not wrong, and not for the sake of being weird like some modern fiddle tunes I've heard. The changes make perfect sense, when you hear them. But you just never *expect* them.

They weren't anything we played on stage regularly, but we fooled around with them a lot when we're just sitting around, playing music for ourselves, so we knew them pretty well. The crowd liked them, too, but once we were through the set, we went back to our regular repertoire until just before we took our break.

"Getting back to fairy folk," I said while Bess got her banjo into a D tuning, "we've got all kinds up in the hills back home. And the funny thing about them is, it turns out they don't necessarily get along with each other any better than we do. This next song kind of borrows the melody of 'Shady Grove,' and it's a love story, but the story it tells is of a feud between the 'sangmen and the bee fairies that also live in our hills."

I played guitar and sang lead on this one, which we'd learned from Sarah Jane. She said she got it from the Apple Tree Man who lives at the back end of her orchard. Seems a 'sangman stole a bee princess away from her hive, but the bee fairies didn't like the idea of one of their highborn ladies living in the dark woods, in a hole in the ground, so they got to feuding. The chorus goes:

> *Once he took her in his arms*
> *and kissed her long and true*
> *Once he took her in his arms*
> *wasn't nothing nobody could do*

I didn't make like we had a personal connection to the song when I was introducing it, but both Bess and I knew it was true because our getting caught up in that generations-long feud is how we ended up being kidnapped by a 'sangman in the first place. The folks listening to the song just followed the story how we told it, but the time or two I glanced in Jim's direction, I could see he was looking thoughtful. I sure hoped it'd make him think about sharing some of his secrets with Bess.

᠊᠊᠊ ᠊᠊᠊ ᠊᠊᠊

I introduced Alice to Bess during the break, explaining how I'd met her in the café, but not what we'd talked about.

"You came all the way up from Tucson to see us?" Bess asked. "How weird is that?"

"It's a nice drive — at least it is after Phoenix."

"But it's so far."

Alice shrugged.

"I came up from Tucson, too," a man said.

We looked over to see a good-looking, dark-haired man standing nearby with one of our CDs in hand. I'd noticed him during the first set, how he'd smiled at me every time we made eye contact. Maybe my luck was changing.

"Really?" I said.

He nodded. "I missed your show at the Hole and I'm going to be out of town when you open for Darlene Flatt, so this was my next closest chance to catch a gig."

"Well, we appreciate you coming so far to see us. Did you want us to sign your CD?"

When he nodded, I handed it to Bess, letting her sign it first.

"Who do you want it made out to?" she asked.

"Alejandro."

She grinned at me because of the way his gaze kept coming back to my face, like it was the needle of a compass and I was due north.

"You should ask him," she said as she handed the CD sleeve to me.

"Ask me what?"

I smiled. "Let me talk to some of these other folks who are waiting, then I'll sign your CD and tell you."

I've noticed that a lot of people are willing to give you a break between sets, waiting for the end of the show to buy CDs or just chat, but there will always be a few who need to talk to you right away. Tonight was no different. Most of the folks here seemed to know each other and were content to chat in small groups, helping themselves to the coffee, tea, and goodies that the Johnsons had laid out, but there were a handful who'd come up as soon as we got off "the stage" — meaning the corner of the room where our gear was set up. I signed their CDs and exchanged a few words, then passed them on to Bess and sat down with Alejandro to sign his CD sleeve.

He thanked me when I handed it back to him, then added, "What did your sister think you should ask me?"

"Do you believe in fairy tales?"

He smiled. "As in are fairies real?"

"Something like that."

He was definitely interested in me, but he seemed genuinely interested in the idea of fairies, too.

"Metaphorically speaking, yes," he said. "I do. I think everything has a spirit and thinking of them as fairies is as good as any other way to be able to talk about them. Of course everyone's going to see them differently, but that's no different from even such a simple thing as language. I mean, how sure can you be that the person you're talking to is really hearing what you're saying? Once it goes through the filter of their preconceptions, a lot can change."

"So you see them as metaphors — not something real."

He shook his head. "The spirit's definitely real. And I'm willing to keep an open mind about the rest of it. But I've never met one the way you said you did when you introduced that first set of tunes tonight."

"Oh, we saw that 'sangman, all right," I said.

"So what was it like?"

"An adventure," I said, remembering. "The kind that's not a whole lot of fun when it's happening, but it's pretty cool when you look back on it."

I knew he wanted more, but then Bess came and tapped me on the shoulder.

"Showtime, Ms. Dillard," she said.

"Okay, I'll be right with you."

I turned back to Alejandro and offered him my hand.

"It was nice to meet you," I said.

"The pleasure was all mine."

His handshake was nice — firm, but not out to prove anything.

"Here," he added, pulling a business card from his pocket. "If you're looking for something to do when you get back to Tucson, give me a call. I can show you around."

"Thanks. Maybe I'll take you up on that."

And then I joined Bess on the "stage" and we started into our second set.

டி டி டி

It got pretty hectic after the encore. A few people already had CDs that they wanted signed and pretty much everybody else wanted to buy one, so we were busy. I saw Alejandro hanging around in back for awhile, but while I smiled and nodded in his direction, I wasn't ready to go out for a drink with him or something. Maybe I would call him when we got back to Tucson, but all I was happy about right now was that a nice-looking guy had sort of hit on me. It restored my confidence.

It's funny. Bess thinks I'm the pretty one, but I don't see it that way at all. We're identical, but if anyone's prettier, if anyone has that special something, she does. She says people are naturally attracted to me, but I always feel like I have to work at it. I don't mean like it's a chore, but I really need my makeup and the right clothes to feel sure of myself. And all my outgoing cheerfulness…it's just a way to cover up my shyness.

Looking good and feeling confident just comes naturally to Bess.

After we packed up our gear, we sat around for awhile with the Johnsons, then Jim took us to the Gurley St. Grill near our hotel for some food and drinks where I worked on convincing Alice to come with us for the rest of our little road trip. When she finally agreed, it was also decided that I'd share her room, leaving the other for the lovebirds.

"I like her," Bess said when we went up to the room to get my stuff.

"Yeah, she's really nice. She's got this calm air about her that makes everything feel okay."

Bess nodded. "She and Jim seem awfully close."

"I think they've known each other forever," I said. "But don't worry. She's married and very much in love with her husband."

"I'm not worried."

"I know you're not," I said, but I thought maybe she was.

Jim really needed to tell her the story about the red dog and the jackalope and I hoped he'd do it soon.

டி டி டி

I rode with Alice in her Forester when we left for Jerome the next morning. The drive was amazing, with spectacular views — especially on the road through Mingus Mountain with the sheer drops on one side or the other of the highway, and the gorgeous panoramas of the mountains and the lower land in between them. And Alice was both good and informative company. Like Jim, she seemed to know everything about the desert and these mountains, but she approached it from a more spiritual perspective, which came from her studying with both spirit and human guides.

It made me wonder if there was something missing in my life. I mean, music's always been a huge part of it, and so has my family, but I've never really thought of myself as a spiritual person and I was wondering if maybe I should. Because something spoke to me in the stories Alice was sharing. It awoke a yearning in me for my own, personal connections to the spirits of the land and all the various beings — human, animal, vegetable — that inhabited it.

And then we started to descend from the mountains into Jerome.

I remember thinking when we first left Prescott that the name of the bar where we were playing seemed so apropos to the conversation that Alice and I were having. It was called the Spirit Room, which had a lovely mystical flavor to it. But of course, by "spirit," they meant booze, which I like as much as the next gal, but it's not the same thing at all.

Jerome was built on the steep side of the mountain, an old mining town given over to the tourist trade, with narrow switchback roads and a lot of greying, ramshackle buildings, but also what seemed like a large number of boutiques, small galleries, restaurants, cafés, and the like. There was even a little storefront museum about copper mining which was the town's lifeblood in the 1800s. And then there was the Spirit Room, housed in a wedge-shaped building with about fifteen motorcycles parked in a line outside.

My heart sank. And sank even further when we went in with our gear because it was a real roadhouse inside with a big dance floor, Christmas lights dangling from where the wood paneling met the green walls, and all those bikers in jeans and leathers, with kerchiefs tied on their heads and their leather bill caps. The women were mostly in tank tops or halters. It was smoky and smelled of fried foods and beer.

But it turned out the bikers were the weekend warrior kind, not Hell's Angels, and there were also some local cowboys and a handful of tourists. And while everybody there was obviously primed for honky-tonk music, they ended up being appreciative of the old-time hillbilly tunes we played. Mind you, we only sold a half-dozen CDs at the end of the show, but at least they listened and even danced some.

Jim was determined that we make the drive to Sedona while it was still light, so after we got paid and had loaded our gear back into the vehicles, off we went again.

The highway took us down from the mountains, back to the desert and into red rock country. I loved the way the big mesas rose up out of the desert, and how their red stone seemed to vibrate against the stands of ponderosa pine and Douglas fir that climbed their lower reaches.

"If you want real drama," Alice said, "you should see the Grand Canyon, but I love this land. It's where I was born."

"So why did you move to Tucson?"

Alice smiled. "You know, I can't even remember anymore. At least, not why I first came. But I know why I stay. For all the medicine wheels and vortexes that Sedona can boast, the Sonoran Desert has a spirit like nowhere else I've been. It twins my heartbeat and enlarges my spirit. Or at least it fills me up."

"I think I know what you mean," I said. "This was home, so you'll always have a connection to it, but Tucson *is* home, the place you can't not live."

"That's exactly it." She glanced at me. "I'm surprised. A lot of people don't get that."

I shrugged. "Maybe they don't feel the magic like we do."

Alice's smile widened. "Yes. If the desert's going to step inside your heart, it happens hard and fast. Does your sister feel the same way?"

"I think so. Of course she's got a whole other reason to be in love with it."

"Ah, yes. Jim's violet eyes."

"The rest of him's not so bad, either."

"No," Alice said. "And his heart's big. But I wish he'd talk to Bess about Corina."

"Yeah. Me, too."

We rode along in silence for awhile, but it wasn't uncomfortable because, like I've already said, Alice has an easy spirit. I just naturally felt relaxed around her — the way I do with my sisters. And then there was the scenery, swallowing my gaze wherever I looked. A cloud cover had rolled in, but even that couldn't spoil my mood.

"Did you know there's a song about how Jim and I met Corina?" Alice asked after awhile.

When I shook my head, she sang it for me, all five verses plus the chorus. She had a surprisingly sweet singing voice that held only a slight trace of the huskiness that was there when she spoke. The chorus was easy for me to pick up and by the end of the song I had a harmony for it.

"So this medicine wheel's where you're meeting up again?" I asked.

Alice nodded. "Though that's not where we met — the song has that wrong. We first met Corina on the slope of Cathedral Rock, which will be coming up on your right in a little bit. But it'll end in the medicine wheel — which is how the wheel got into the song, I suppose."

"Who wrote it?"

"I'm not sure. It's been around a long time."

⌐ ⌐ ⌐

The afternoon was easing into the evening before we finally got to Sedona itself. I'd booked us a room at the White House Inn, way back when we first got the gig, and it turned out to be easy to find because it was right on Hwy 89A, which we were already on as we came into town. We checked in, taking an extra room for Alice and myself so that the lovebirds could have one to themselves again. We couldn't get adjoining rooms, but they were on top of each other, so Alice and I were on the second floor with Bess and Jim directly below us. The place didn't have the charm of the Hotel St. Michael back in Prescott — it was a highway motel, after all — but it was cheaper, with big, clean rooms and great views. At least, Alice and I had a great view. Because of our second floor elevation, we could look past the highway in front and the parking lot in back and see those red stone mesas.

Having been so long in the car — looking at, but not able to be *in* the landscape — we all wanted to walk a little bit in the desert before we had dinner. So even though it was starting to get dark now, we all piled into the Forester and Alice drove us through a bewildering maze of residential streets near the motel until we finally came out at a trailhead and pulled into its small parking lot. I hadn't insisted that we freshen up first, like I usually do when we arrive in a new place, and I'm glad I didn't, because we were just in time to catch the tail-end of the sunset.

The cloud cover stole the big light show we might have gotten otherwise, but there's still something about twilight that always makes everything look magical and this little piece of desert was no exception. Bess and Jim walked ahead of us on the trail. I heard a caw and looked up to see three crows, playing together in the last light. Alice raised a hand and waved to them and I swear each of them dipped a wing in response before flying off.

"Do you know them?" I asked.

Alice shook her head. "But they're cousins, so they're able to recognize me."

I remembered Jim talking about cousins on that first hike we'd done in the Tucson Mountains. Now it made more sense.

Bess and Jim had stopped up ahead.

"I think we should go back," Bess said. "It's getting so I can't see where I'm putting my feet, though Jim here seems to be able to see in the dark."

"It's a healthy diet," he said. "Lots of carrots."

Oh, just tell her, I thought. But of course he couldn't, not with all of us here.

� ⌐ ⌐

We had dinner at a place called El Rincon. I wasn't expecting much when I heard it was in a mall, but the mall was like some oversized hacienda and the restaurant had a lovely, welcoming atmosphere — not to mention great margaritas of which we all had perhaps too many, except for Alice. We sat on the patio with blankets on our knees against the night's chill. Jim and Alice entertained us with stories of some of the desert rat characters they knew in a way that included Bess and me instead of the way some old friends reminisce, which leaves you without much of a clue as to what they're talking about.

When we got back to the motel, I asked Alice to write out the words to that song she'd sung for me in the car on the way to Sedona. I had an idea how I might use it if Jim didn't open up to Bess soon.

⌐ ⌐ ⌐

I called the Chases when I got up the next morning — these were the people putting on tonight's house concert. Nathan and Judy Chase. I got Judy and she asked if we could be there by seven so that we could be set up before people started to arrive. I said okay, grinning when I hung up, because that meant we had the whole day to ourselves. Alice and I went down the road to the Ravenheart Café and brought back coffees and muffins for the slug-a-beds downstairs, then we sat around making plans. It was overcast again, with the odd spit of rain, but we were determined to get in some hiking.

Alice wanted us to see Oak Creek and both she and Jim said that we had to at least hike partway up Cathedral Rock, so as soon as we were done with breakfast we set out in the Forester. I understood their enthusiasm when we pulled into the parking lot at Oak Creek.

We could see Cathedral Rock rearing up, red and dramatic, on the other side of the creek, with a skirt of pine and fir climbing partway up its height from the base. The sky was a dark swirl of clouds behind the summit. I actually felt something tug in my chest at the sight of it all — I'm not sure what. A need to go there, but something else, as well. Something I couldn't explain except as a yearning for...more. More what, I don't know. It was a bit like I felt in that art exhibit Jim had taken us to in Tucson, but even more intense.

But where the distant rock was dramatic, the banks of the creek filled me with peace. The weather was keeping most of the other tourists away, so we pretty much had the area to ourselves, which only added to the mood. And it was so pretty. The water ran over a bed of pebbles and the banks were thick with willows, oaks, and those gorgeous sycamores that I remembered from Sabino Canyon. They were Alice's tree, I remembered Jim saying. Maybe that was why she was so happy here, except I was happy, too.

Because of the rains they'd been getting, the creek was swollen and we couldn't find a place to cross over.

"That's okay," Alice said. "We can drive around to the trailhead on the other side."

So we started back to the parking lot. Bess fell in beside me and linked her arm in mine.

"I've been missing you," she said.

I smiled. "I'm right beside you."

"You know what I mean. It's not the same, waking up with you in a different room, morning after morning. You're not feeling too third-wheely are you?"

I shook my head. "No. I'm happy for you, and I'm enjoying Alice's company."

"Yeah, she seems like a pretty neat lady."

"But?" I prompted, knowing her too well.

I can always tell when she's not saying everything on her mind. She shot a look behind to where Alice and Jim were walking.

"I don't know. They seem pretty close."

"But it's not smoochy-close the way you and he are. I told you. They just go way back, that's all."

"I guess," she said. "But there's something more between them. Some kind of...I don't know. Secret."

"I wouldn't worry about that," I said. "I think they're the poster people for secrets."

But now she was the one to give me the knowing look.

"There's something going on with you," she said, "but I can't figure out what it is. Are you *sure* you're okay with all of this?"

Except for the fact that I knew more about her boyfriend than she did and it was killing me?

"I'm fine," I told her. "I guess it's like you were saying. It's weird waking with Alice in the room instead of you, but I don't want to change it. I *like* that you've found this guy."

She gave a slow nod. "But what am I going to do with him?"

"Let it go at its own pace," I said.

She nodded again and then we were back at the car and the others had joined us.

ᒣ ᒣ ᒣ

It wasn't far to the trailhead. Because of the continuing overcast skies and the odd sprinkles of rain, there weren't many people here either. I spotted only two other cars in the parking lot when we pulled in.

"It smells so good here," Bess said when we got out of the car.

I knew what she meant. There was a tang in the air, something the damp was bringing out of the vegetation and the red dirt underfoot.

She and Jim took the lead again. Alice and I fell behind, walking slower.

"So is it weird being here?" I asked as the path climbed in among the evergreens.

"Why would it be weird?"

I shrugged. "Well, this is where the curse started, isn't it?"

"I don't think of it as a curse," she said. "And I doubt Jim does, either. We were woken to so much on that day."

"I guess."

Bess and Jim were pretty far ahead of us. I paused to look at the view. Red rock formations went on forever, broken by stands of tall Douglas fir and the ponderosa pines.

"I can give you a hint of what it's like," Alice said.

I turned to look at her.

"And no," she added before I could ask. "It won't change you. At least, not physically. But it might put a yearning in your heart."

I smiled. "I've always got a yearning in my heart. I don't know for what, just something."

"Take my hand," she said.

I did, not sure what to expect, or what she did, but everything around us shimmered for a long moment. I blinked and had to lean against Alice, feeling a small wave of nausea.

"Oh, I'm sorry," she said. "I forgot that there can be a bit of vertigo when you first cross over. It's different for everybody and it's usually worse when you cross all the way over into *huya aniya* — what my friend Bettina calls *la época del mito,* the place of myth time."

"Cross over?" I repeated.

"Into the spiritworld."

"That's where we are?"

She shook her head. "No, this is *el entre,* the place between the world we live in and *huya aniya,* the world of the spirits."

I stood on my own now, the nausea gone, and looked around.

"It doesn't look any different," I began, but then realized that wasn't entirely right.

It was no different, but at the same time, it was entirely different. Everything had more...presence. The big slab of red rock underfoot. The fir trees that reared above us. And then, when I turned to look at Alice, I saw the small horns on her brow, the rabbit ears lying alongside her head like two braids. It was like the momentary glimpse I'd had in the café, except this time it wasn't here and then gone again. She was really standing there, half human, half something magical.

"You..."

She laughed. "Don't look any different?"

I just shook my head and took a deep breath.

"Everything's different," I said. "It feels like you could live on this air. And it's all..." I waved my hand to take in the trees, the rocks, everything around us.

"Vibrating."

Alice nodded. She took my hand and the view shimmered once more.

She didn't have to say we were back. I could feel it — a pang of disappointment that lodged deep in my chest. Everything seemed flat and Alice was just Alice again.

"When I was a jackalope," she said. "Before Corina changed us. I only knew one world, too."

"I get it," I said. "It's not a curse. It was a gift. Even if it has an expiry date."

"Exactly."

"But even a hundred years ago," I said. "Wouldn't a jackalope still be pretty magical? I mean, I always thought they were a taxidermist's joke — you know, stick some little antelope antlers on a jackrabbit and pretend that it's real."

She nodded. "When I said I only knew one world, I didn't mean this one."

"Ah. I get it."

And I did. What I'd just experienced was this huge swell of knowledge that was filling me, from toe tip to the top of my head. And I understood what Alice had meant about it not changing me physically, but changing me all the same. Or maybe not changing me, so much as reminding me of what I'd already experienced once before when Bess and I were kidnapped into fairyland. I'd forgotten the immediacy of the feeling, how it made you look at everything with different eyes.

"Come on," Alice said. "We should catch up with the others."

Bess gave me a funny look when we joined them up on this huge expanse of red stone with a view that seemed to go on forever.

"It's okay," I told her. I couldn't pretend that nothing had happened, because she had to have felt something. "I just got this weird flash of vertigo."

She gave me a hug.

"I knew it was something," she said. "For a moment it was like you'd just disappeared off the face of the earth. I couldn't feel you *anywhere.*"

I caught the look Jim gave Alice, but none of us said anything.

"I'm fine now," I said instead. "Wow, would you look at this view?"

当 当 当

When we got back to the motel, I looked up the Chases' address on one of the roadmaps Alice had in her car and found it was near the end of Coyote Drive, in the same maze of streets we'd had to navigate last night when we'd been looking for the trailhead. We put our gear in the back of the Forester and off we went to find it.

It turned out to be a long bungalow surrounded by evergreens and getting there was a lot easier than it had been trying to find the trailhead last night. Maybe because this time we'd actually looked at the map first. John Chase was nice enough, if a little standoffish, but Judy's exuberance more than made up for that. She was one of those small women with an excess of energy and a great laugh that we got to hear a lot, because pretty much everything seemed to make her laugh.

The room they'd set up for the concert was a big, kind of family room off the kitchen which made for easy access to the coffee, tea and a whole countertop of snacks: cut vegetables and dips, tortilla chips and several different kinds of salsas, cookies and brownies and muffins. It looked like they were expecting to feed an army.

The turnout was a little more modest than that, but we did have a full house again, which surprised me, what with Monday being a "school night" and all. I counted thirty-eight people — including Jim and Alice and our hosts — and they proved to be an appreciative bunch, which always makes for a great gig. The positive feedback cranks us up, making us play better, which in turn makes the audience give us even more energy and the whole thing spirals up into a state where everybody's feeling a little delirious.

The first set was really good, but the second went so well that both Bess and I were feeling positively giddy as we came up to its finish. We'd planned to end with our usual high-energy finish: a pair of fast Stanley Brothers' tunes, then the "Hey! Ho! Let's go!" chant from the Ramones' "Blitzkrieg Bop" as a bridge leading into a bluegrass-fast cover of "Jersey Devil" by Kevin Welch. But before Bess could retune her banjo for the set, I exchanged my fiddle for the guitar.

Bess gave me a puzzled look.

"I've got a new song," I told her. "In A minor. Want to give it a go?"

"Sure," she said. "Have I heard it before?"

I shook my head. "I just learned it today."

I knew she was about to ask me from where, so I turned to face the audience before she could.

"We've got time for a couple more pieces," I said, "and one of them's a song my poor sister's never even heard before. We do this to each other all the time — it keeps us on our toes."

That got a bigger chuckle than it deserved, so I turned to have a look, and sure enough, Bess was getting the laugh by standing on her tippy-toes and pretending to have to work at keeping her balance. I, in turn, pretended to be annoyed, but could only just keep the smile twitching at my lips from turning into a full-blown grin.

"Anyway," I said, "this is another traditional piece, but it comes from right here in Sedona. And supposedly it's a true story."

With that, I launched into the song Alice had sung for me in the car. This time I got a reaction from Jim. I saw him sit up straight, then shoot a quick look at Alice, who only shrugged in response. When his gaze returned to me, I smiled and knew he got it.

"That's a cool song," Bess said as she retuned her banjo for our final piece.

"Thanks."

She waited a beat, but when I didn't elaborate, she shrugged and set the pace for the Stanley Brothers' reel that started our last set of tunes.

ᒲ ᒲ ᒲ

Later, back at the motel, I turned to Alice after we'd both had a shower and were getting ready for bed.

"So now we find out," I said. "Or rather, Bess does."

She nodded. "Jim didn't say anything to me, but I think he's relieved that you forced his hand."

"God, I hope it goes well. What if my forcing the issue screws everything up?"

"It had to come out into the open," she said. "Better sooner than later."

"Yeah, but..."

"It's done," Alice said, "and we can't take it back. All we can do is go to sleep and hope for the best when we wake up in the morning."

"I guess."

Alice turned out the light and got under the covers. I looked over at what I could see of her bed in the dark. She was taking her own advice.

Easy for her, I thought, as I slid down from where I'd been leaning against the headboard and got under my own covers. It's not her sister that's down there, finding out she's been dating some kind of dog man.

I was sure I'd never get to sleep. But I couldn't sense any distress coming from Bess, and we'd had a long day of hiking, followed by a really great gig — which always leaves me exhilarated right after, but then I crash big time a couple of hours later. I guess it all caught up to me, because one moment I was staring at the ceiling and the next thing I knew, I was lunging out of a deep sleep — feeling panicky, with my heart beating way too fast and no idea as to what had woken me.

The radio clock told me it was almost five A.M. I looked at Alice's bed, but it was empty. Before that could really register, I realized that the panic I was feeling wasn't my own. It was an echo I was picking up from Bess.

Bess!

I jumped out of bed, threw a jean jacket on over the long T-shirt I was using for a nightie, and was out the door without even stopping to think about what I was doing. My bare feet slapped on the cool flooring of the balcony as I ran for the stairs down to the room Bess was sharing with Jim.

I found her at the bottom of the stairs, huddled up against the railing and crying. I gave the parking lot a once-over as I hurried to her side, but both Jim's pickup and the Forester were still in their spots.

"Oh, Bess," I said. I sat down beside her and put my arms around her. "What happened?"

It took her a few moments just to string some words together that made sense.

"I don't...I don't even know where to start," she finally managed. "It's like that whole business with Sarah Jane all over again." She turned to face me, cheeks glistening in the glow from the parking lot's lights. "You know...all the way past weird to freak-out land."

"We got through that," I reminded her.

"Yeah, but he's a dog, Laurel. I didn't know what to think when he started off telling me about all of this, but then, just before he left, he actually turned into this big red dog. I thought I'd die."

"I know," I said. "A spirit dog."

"What do you mean, 'you know'? You knew and you didn't tell me?"

"It's complicated."

"No shit."

"You guys were getting along so well —"

"Yeah, but he's a *dog!*"

"And I didn't want to be the one to screw everything up."

She shook her head. "I don't see how it could be any more screwed up."

"I thought it'd be different if he told you."

"It was different all right."

"What did he say to you? Why did he leave?"

"He left because I told him to get the hell out." She wiped at her eyes and stared across the darkened parking lot. "And as for what he said...well, I guess you already know." She paused, looked back at me. *"How* do you know?"

"I met Ramona in the café in Prescott — just before I met Alice. She told me first, and then Alice confirmed it."

"Alice." Bess gave a slow shake of her head. "I knew there was something creepy between the two of them."

"There's nothing going on between them," I said. "She's got a husband she loves."

"Yeah, and a deal with this Coyote Woman —"

"Corina."

"Whatever. But it all centers around me becoming some kind of love slave to him. Maybe to both of them."

"Is that what he said?"

"No, but he might as well have. They both get turned back into animals unless he gets someone to fall in love with him."

I didn't see where that translated into her becoming a "love slave," but I knew she wasn't thinking clearly, so I didn't push it.

"I think he really does care about you," I said instead.

"Well, sure. Just like if you're drowning, you get real fond of whoever throws you a line."

"You know it isn't like that."

"No, I don't. How could I?"

"Your heart —"

"Was so ga-ga I couldn't think straight."

I shook my head. "Alice says —"

"Alice. God, she's as bad as he is."

I raised an eyebrow.

"Well, think about it," Bess said. "She has just as much to lose as he does, so of course she's going to come along and do her bit to try to win me over."

"When did she do that?"

"I don't know. She didn't. But why else would she have come along?"

"Because I asked her to. I had to *talk* her into it — remember?"

"Oh, whose side are you on anyway?"

"Yours," I said without hesitation. "Always yours. So this is your call. Whatever you want to do, that's what we'll do."

"I never want to see either of them again," Bess said.

"Okay. Except we need to get back to Tucson and Greyhound doesn't run a line between here and there."

"So we'll take the pickup. Jim can ride back with his girlfriend."

I guess it was understandable that she'd be so fixated on that, and I wished there was a way I could convince her otherwise, but I didn't see that happening any time soon. I also wished I'd told her myself. Maybe I could have done it in a way that wouldn't have gotten her so upset. I don't know. But it was too late for any of that. Right now, I was here to support her, no questions. That's what we always did for each other.

"Okay," I said. "We take the pickup. Do you know where they've gone?"

She shook her head. "I watched him — the dog — run to the highway and then I heard Alice call to him from the balcony up above. He changed back into Jim and waited for her and they had some kind of argument, I guess. And then the two of them just vanished."

"You mean they went somewhere."

"No, they just disappeared."

I gave a slow nod. "Into the spiritworld."

"How do you know *that?*"

"Alice showed it to me yesterday, when we were hiking up to Cathedral Rock."

"I hate this," Bess said. "It really is like what happened back home, isn't it? On Aunt Lillian's farm."

"I guess. Except there's no war going on here. There's just a red dog who fell in love with you too late for it to do anybody good."

"Don't say it like that..."

"Okay, but I have to ask you. If all of this freaks you out so much, why have you kept on asking people if they believe in fairy tales?"

"Because you wanted us to."

"But —"

"And this is *so* different. It's not being in a fairyland for a day or so and then everything's back to normal again. This is falling for some guy who turns out to be some kind of fairy tale were-dog and you know that if you let him stick around, you're going to have to deal with all of this for the whole rest of your life. I can't do that, Laurel. I just can't, so don't...don't ask me to..."

I started to say, "Sorry," but she was already crying again, so I held her until the worst was over. I waited until her tears subsided, then dug a pretty clean tissue out of the pocket of my jean jacket and gave it to her to blow her nose.

"We should pack up and go," I said. "Before they get back. Unless..?"

"No. I want to go."

Alice

Alice came awake the way she always did — one moment she was fast asleep, the next she was completely alert. She lay still, listening for what had woken her, then realized it hadn't been a sound, but a feeling. A cousin had shifted into animal shape nearby — a hunter — and the jackalope in her had immediately become aware of possible danger.

Coyote, she thought.

No. But definitely a canid.

And then she recognized the familiar whisper of his spirit.

It was Jim.

She rose soundlessly from the bed and got dressed. A glance at the other bed told her Laurel was still sleeping. Picking up her wool jacket with its Navajo patterning, she slipped out the door.

The red dog that was Jim was already across the parking lot by the highway. She called his name as she put on her jacket and he turned. At first she didn't think he'd wait for her, but he was still there, rising up to stand as a five-fingered being by the time she reached him.

"What happened?" she asked.

A world of pain swam in his eyes.

But, "Go home," was all he said. "Go back to Thomas. Take what you can out of the few days we have left."

"Where are you going? What *happened?*"

He shrugged, rolled a cigarette and lit it. "Nothing. Everything. I wasn't who she thought I was supposed to be, so she threw me out."

Alice put a hand on his arm. "Oh, Jim. I'm so sorry."

"Don't be. This is all my fault. But it's kind of ironic — don't you think? — that after a hundred years I finally find a woman I can love, but it's far too late to do any of us any good."

"You told her everything?"

He nodded. "What was I supposed to do? What with that song you coached Laurel to sing last night."

"I didn't tell her to —"

"It doesn't matter," Jim broke in. "It's all over now. You should really go back to Tucson and spend these last few days with Thomas."

Alice shook her head. "Not until you tell me where you're going."

She didn't think he would answer, and for a long moment he didn't. He looked away, across the highway, finishing his cigarette. Dropping the butt on the pavement, he ground it out with his boot, then stooped to pick it up and stow it in his pocket.

"Jim?"

He sighed and turned back to her.

"I'm going to the medicine wheel," he said. "To see Corina."

"But why? It's not time yet."

"So? A few days isn't going to make any difference to me. Not now. But it can to you. That's why I'm telling you to go back to Thomas."

"No. I can't just —"

He put his hand on her shoulder. "I'm really sorry, Alice. I didn't mean for it to turn out this way. But I never met my Thomas until Bess came into my life. It wasn't that I was unwilling to commit before this. Honestly. There was just nobody I wanted to commit to."

"You can't just give up," Alice said.

"You didn't see the look in her eyes. Nothing I can do or say will change the way she feels."

"You have to try."

He shook his head.

"I'm not saying this for me," she told me. "I'm saying it for you. You can't just give up on this — not if you feel as strongly about her as you say you do."

"There isn't the time."

"But —"

"It's just the way it worked out," he said. "I'm sorry, Alice. Now go back to Thomas — spend what time you have left with him. God knows I would, if I had someone to go back to."

"What will you tell Corina?"

"Being Corina, I probably don't have to tell her anything. She'll already know."

Alice shook her head. "No. She's an old spirit, but she can't see inside our hearts, can she?"

"It doesn't matter," he said. "You should just go home and let me worry about it."

"I can't. I can't just leave you to do this on your own. We're supposed to go there together."

"What about Thomas?"

Alice thought of the years she'd had with Thomas and compared them to the few days Jim had managed with Bess. And then she thought of what Jim had been through all those years. All this time she'd thought he was simply being frivolous — he'd certainly acted that way. But now she knew it was only because he hadn't met "his Thomas," as he'd put it. He'd put a cocky face to the world to hide the hurt, but he'd still had to carry that hurt for all these years. Carry it by himself. And she knew how hard that was, because she'd carried the same loneliness for seventy years herself, until she finally met Thomas.

"I'm not letting you do this alone," she said.

He regarded her for a long moment, seeing she didn't know what in her features. She hoped it wasn't pity. She hoped it was the understanding she'd gained, and the simple truth that while they could never be a couple, she would always love him.

Finally, he gave a slow nod.

"I'd be honored to have your company," he told her.

It was the most formal thing she'd ever heard him say.

She wanted to hug him. She wanted to shoulder all the loneliness and hurt he'd had to carry on his own for so long.

"How were you planning to go?" she asked instead.

"Through *el entre*. It's quicker than driving."

She nodded. "But I don't think I can keep up with a red dog."

"We'll go as we are — a last trip as five-fingered beings."

🔲 🔲 🔲

Alice let him lead the way into *el entre* and then out again. They emerged onto a narrow trail that ran alongside a low canyon wall of massive rock outcrops, startling a small herd of javelinas. Alice wrinkled her nose at their smell, but smiled as they trotted to safety. There was something too amusing about how bulky they appeared until you faced them head-on, and then they were like mobile cardboard cutouts.

They followed the sandy trail as it wound through agave, yucca, and other desert shrubs heading for the towering sandstone cliffs that lay ahead. By the last few stars in the dawning sky, Alice could tell that they were somewhere northeast of the motel now, walking in a few minutes what would otherwise have taken them a couple of hours. To the left of the trail she noticed a number of buildings behind a six-foot-high adobe wall.

"It's a resort," Jim said as they passed a gate in the wall that gave access to the place. "We'll be past it soon."

Alice nodded.

The trail took them past the resort to the mouth of the canyon. Once inside, it followed a creek across the canyon floor. The red and buff canyon walls began to rise on either side, growing steeper the further in they went. The creek bed was damp, but there wasn't any water in it except for the odd small puddle. Patches of wildflowers appeared among the shrubs. Further in, the creek bed widened and vegetation grew taller, a mix of oak and juniper and pine. They could hear a dawn chorus of pinyon jays, deeper in the canyon.

"You know what my biggest mistake was?" Jim said.

His voice startled Alice. She'd been so absorbed with her surroundings that she'd almost forgotten whom she was with and why they were here.

"What was that?" she asked.

But brought back as she was, she knew immediately what was on his mind, probably because the Dillard sisters were on hers now as well.

"Telling Bess about her own cousin blood," he said. "I think that scared her more than learning what I am."

"But it's not strong — did you tell her that?"

He shook his head.

"Why not? It might have helped."

"You've been with them," he said. "It's strong enough to wake. I wasn't going to pretend otherwise. We'd already had enough lies."

"So you told her that?"

"No. I just didn't bring it up."

"They're different in that respect," Alice told him. "Laurel seems quite intrigued with the idea of shapechanging and cousins. I took her into *el entre* yesterday — just briefly."

"I noticed. I think Bess did, too — they have as much of an awareness of each other as we cousins do. But she wouldn't have known what she was feeling."

"Just that her sister was gone."

Jim nodded. "So how did Laurel take it?"

"She had a touch of vertigo, but otherwise she was fine." Alice smiled. "Actually, she loved it."

"Maybe I should have tried that with Bess."

"Not without some forewarning. Don't forget, Laurel and I have been talking about this since I first met her in Prescott."

"Yeah, you're right. It probably wouldn't have made any difference, anyway."

The oaks and pines were thicker now and tall enough to block their view of the sandstone cliffs. The trail crossed back and forth over the creek as it twisted down through the canyon like a snake. The creek bed was wider here than it had been earlier, choked with rounded stones and pebbles. On the damp sand of its banks they left the imprints of their boots in among the tracks of ringtail cats, coyotes, deer, and other animals. Ferns grew under the trees, tall patches that swayed with the morning breeze. Above the forest canopy, the sky grew lighter. When the sun broke over the rim on the canyon, they found themselves walking through cathedralling shafts of light. They could still hear the jays, closer now, and then they came to a clearing.

They stopped and looked down at the medicine wheel.

It filled the clearing, twenty-five feet or so across, the circle and crossing lines built up of stones and small boulders piled almost two feet high. On the far side of the medicine wheel, the land opened up again and they could catch glimpses of the canyon walls, far off past the tops of the trees.

"It's so beautiful here," Alice murmured.

"You sound surprised."

She turned to look at him. "I am. I guess I shouldn't be. But I was always scared to come here..."

"Because this is where it ends for us."

She nodded.

"I was scared, too," he said. "At least the first few times. But I kept having this morbid need to see it for myself. And then whenever I got here..." He let his hands speak for him, moving them to encompass everything around them. "I come here all the time now. Not *here* exactly, not to the medicine wheel. But to this canyon. There's this place...let me show you."

He took her hand and led her around the medicine wheel to where the trail continued up the canyon for another half mile. From there it was a rough scramble on loose stones until, two-thirds up the wall of the canyon, they found a narrow footpath that followed the cliff wall back for another quarter of a mile or so before it ended. On the other side of what would be a three-foot jump, a large, flat rock stood free of the cliff.

Jim made the jump first, then looked back at her.

"Can you make it okay?" he asked.

Alice smiled at him. "Jackalope — remember?"

"Right."

But he still caught her arm when she landed, letting go only when he was sure she had her balance.

"This is perfect," she said as she took in the view.

They sat on the rock and looked out over the canyon. Jim rolled a cigarette and offered it to her. She let him light it for her and took a puff, then handed it back to him. Putting away his tobacco, he accepted the cigarette from her.

There was no sign of the modern world here, only the canyon walls on either side, red and buff. Far below, Alice saw that the trail they'd been following continued only a short way up the canyon where it ended in a tumble of giant rocks and red dirt. The other way, she could only see the swaying green tops of the forest they'd just walked through.

The sun was higher now, the sky a perfect clear blue. A hawk floated by, dipping its wings in greeting before continuing up the canyon. Later a pair of ravens did the same.

"I could stay here forever," Alice said after they'd been there awhile.

"Maybe you should stay."

"Don't start that again," she told him.

"No, I'm serious. We're not supposed to be here for another week or so. Why should you come down there with me?"

"We got into this together. We'll finish it the same way."

He looked as though he might continue his argument, but instead he only nodded.

"Which we should probably do now," she added.

They were slower returning to the clearing. When they reached the canyon floor, Jim turned to look back the way they'd come.

"I was thinking," he said, returning his attention to her. "Isn't there some story about how your life can get all messed up when you start hanging around with deer women?"

Alice nodded. He was thinking about the Dillard sisters again and their weak cousin blood.

"But it's not a desert story," she said, "and nothing that's happened here is deliberate, the way it is in that story."

"Doesn't stop it from hurting."

"No. I doubt there's a cure for that."

He sighed and led the way back towards the forest.

"Maybe she won't be here," he said. "I mean, just because we're early, doesn't mean she will be."

But when they reached the clearing, they saw a tall figure waiting for them, wrapped in a dark blanket, standing barefoot in the center of the medicine wheel. She had coyote features under her black, flat-brimmed hat, dark braids falling down either side of her head.

Corina.

Alice didn't know if Jim was feeling the same second thoughts as she was, but it was too late now anyway. They were here. Coyote Woman was here. All that remained was to finish the story.

Laurel

It didn't take us long to gather our things and load them into Jim's pickup.

"I hate Sedona," Bess said as we stood in the parking lot, watching the dawn pink the eastern horizon.

"No, you don't."

"No, I don't," she agreed. "It just feels like I should."

I went back inside the motel room I'd shared with Alice to have a last look around. I rarely forget something, but I can't stop myself from checking all the same. Bess followed me inside and objected when I left a note for Alice. I did it anyway.

"You know I'm going to spend some time with Alice when we get back to Tucson," I said.

Bess nodded. "I wouldn't stop you." Then she sighed. "It's too bad. I really liked her — I know what you're thinking," she added. "But I did, even if I couldn't help but feel a little jealous about this secret they had going between them. It's weird. The way I feel now, I almost wish that they *had* been romantically involved. It'd make it easier to be mad at them."

I hesitated a moment, then felt I had to say it.

"He never lied to you," I told her. "He just didn't tell you everything. You know it's not the same thing."

"It doesn't matter. It doesn't change what he is."

I felt my patience running a little thin.

"So," I asked. "Is this like when Buck found out that Jeremy's gay?"

Buck and Jeremy were neighbors of ours, back home in Tyson County. They'd been best friends all through grade and high school and Jeremy had never hit on Buck — and he wasn't hitting on him when he outted himself. But Buck just shut him out of his life all the same. When I asked him why he couldn't be friends with Jeremy anymore, all he could give me for an answer was, "Jesus. He's a queer. How am I supposed to get over something like *that?*"

"This is so different," Bess said. "Jim and Alice...they're, you know...animals..."

"Would you feel the same if it was someone in our family? If it was me, or Mama?"

"We would never choose to be something like that."

I wasn't so sure about that, but it wasn't something I wanted to get into right now.

"Neither did they," I told her, instead. "They're like Jeremy. It's just the way they are."

Tears welled in her eyes. "Don't...don't make me out to be the bad guy..."

"I'm sorry," I said. And I really was. "I'm being an idiot. You don't need to hear any of that."

She shook her head. "I...I understand what you're saying, Laurel. I do. But it's just...too hard right now."

I put my arm around her shoulders and gave her a hug, then steered her from the motel room. I made sure the door locked behind us. Outside the sun was above the horizon now and the sky was a clear blue for as far as we could see in any direction. It was going to make for a gorgeous drive back to Tucson — so long as Jim didn't report his pickup as having been stolen and we got pulled over by state troopers.

But I didn't mention that worry to Bess. We got into Jim's truck, buckled up, and then we were off.

I was surprised at how well the pickup handled. I'd ridden in it before, of course, but this was my first time behind the wheel. I'd expected it to be a little clunky. Instead, it was like driving some high-end car. Either Jim was one hell of a mechanic, or he'd laid a bit of his otherworld magic on it. I smiled to myself. Maybe I was really driving a Jag or BMW and it just *looked* like a beat-up old pickup, the way a red dog could look like a man.

I didn't mention that to Bess either. I doubted she was ready for any kind of jokes right now, but for sure not ones about shapechanging anythings, never you mind trucks.

"So," I said when we'd been on the road for awhile. "Is it going to bother you having to hang around Tucson for the rest of the week?"

Our gig opening for Darlene wasn't until Friday and today was only Monday.

Bess shook her head. "I'm not letting what happened with Jim spoil how I feel about this area. I like it around here too much."

"Me, too. I could *totally* live in the desert."

That actually pulled a tiny bit of a smile from Bess and I knew just what she was thinking.

When we first started traveling, pretty much any place we toured, we wanted to pack up all of our stuff and immediately move there. We soon figured out that it was only the tourist syndrome, how being free of all your usual responsibilities adds this extra sheen to an already exotic locale — exotic, for us, being any place that wasn't the hills where we grew up. Though we had gigs, which made us working girls instead of just tourists, we were still susceptible to it, even now, when we knew better.

But this was different. This wasn't a momentary infatuation, born of the tourist syndrome glamor. This landscape was speaking right to our hearts — at least it was to mine. Something here was reaching right into my soul and — oh, I don't know. It was like I was saying to Alice on the drive from Jerome.

I felt like I'd come home.

🔲 🔲 🔲

Bess slept for most of the trip back to Tucson, but I didn't mind. The drive to Phoenix was gorgeous and though I was driving, I still got to drink it in — all these vast sweeps of desert backed by dramatic rock formations and red limestone bluffs. Just being able to look out at the landscape filled me with a peace I'd never gotten from my surroundings before. It was funny. If anyone had asked me before we got here, I would never have guessed that I'd fall in love with these badlands.

I'll never understand how they came to be known as badlands. Well, I do, of course. It's because it's not good for crops or grazing, so it's "bad land." But that's such a blinkered perspective. A better name would be spirit lands, because they're so full of spirits. I know every place has spirit, but maybe the reason it's so strong here is because we work so hard at driving the spirits away from everywhere else with our housing projects and industries and clearcutting and all, these are the only places left to them now.

We managed to get through the city without getting caught in the worst of its morning rush hour, but the drive from Phoenix to Tucson was just as boring as it had been on the way going, except this time I was the one who had to deal with all the big tractor trailers on the freeway — a big not fun. Bess woke up when we reached Tucson and helped me navigate our way off the freeway and through the tangle of one-way streets back to the Hotel Congress.

We lucked out at the hotel. I thought we'd have to wait for a room until later in the day, but they had one free for us. We unpacked the pickup and I parked it in the overflow parking lot across Toole Avenue, right beside the warehouse building housing the artists' studios and the gallery Jim had taken us to the other day. When I got back to our room, Bess was lying on the bed. She wasn't crying, but she had that exhaustion that depression brings.

I sat down on the bed beside her and stroked her forehead, pushing the hair back from her face.

"I wish there was something I could do to make you feel better," I said.

"Yeah. Me, too."

"Do you want me to get you a tea or something from the café?"

She gave a little shake of her head. "I'm going to try to sleep. You must be tired, too, after all that driving."

"No, I'm kind of super awake."

"You don't have to stay with me."

"I know. But I'll wait to see if you fall asleep."

She was still protesting that I didn't need to when she drifted off.

I sat there watching her sleep for a long time, feeling worse and worse for what I'd done. None of this would be happening if I hadn't pushed Jim to talk to her about his secrets. What business was it of mine what they did and didn't tell each other? Bess probably hadn't told him about our own visit to fairyland. But now everything was wrong and final and she had this big weird thing going on about what I thought were amazing things. The spiritlands. Magic. Connecting with the animal spirits inside us.

How could any of that freak her out? It wasn't like Jim was some gnarly 'sangman, ready to stick us in a hole in the ground the way our last experience in fairyland had gone. He and Alice were wonderful. They hadn't suddenly become monsters. But try convincing Bess of that. She really was being just as bad as Buck, for all the same dumb reasons.

If there was only some way I could convince her that...

I don't know where the idea came from, the way it did — sudden and completely formed in my head.

But I knew what I had to do.

Ramona

Ramona was in a bar near the Yaqui pueblo on the west side of Tucson, drinking tequila. She had a bottle on her table and every time her glass was empty, she mechanically filled it again. The trouble was, she couldn't get drunk.

She couldn't forget.

Usually, in a place such as this, she radiated charm, drawing men to her like the flowers of red beardtongue draw hummingbirds. But today she let enough of the snake in her show that no one approached her table. No one even considered it.

Until he was there.

"<Congratulations, Ramona,>" Jorge said.

She looked up at him, eyes narrowed.

"<You didn't hear?>" he went on. "<A jay told me the news. How Changing Dog and his red-haired girlfriend have had a falling out, and now both he and Corn Hair have gone to meet Corina at the wheel. A week and a half early.>"

"<Jays are gossips and liars,>" Ramona told him.

"Some, perhaps," Jorge said, switching to English. "But not this one. I mean, he likes to gossip, but he doesn't tell lies. He was there, in Sedona. He saw it happen."

"And so he flew all the way here to tell you."

"No. I met him in *el entre*."

Ramona nodded. Of course. Where distance didn't have the same meaning as it did in this world.

She swallowed her shot in one gulp, then poured herself another.

"You don't seem happy," Jorge said. "And you're not sharing."

"Get your own bottle," she told him. "And what do I have to be happy about?"

Jorge shrugged. "But isn't this what you wanted?"

Ramona raised her gaze to his, her yellow snake-eyes shiny.

"I don't know what I want anymore," she said. "But I know it's not this."

"I don't understand."

"I met Rosa. In Prescott."

"Ah."

Ramona shook her head. "No, it's not like what you think. She didn't warn me off or put a hex on me or anything."

"Then what?"

"I don't know. She had nothing in her hands, but somehow she held a mirror up to me and all I could see was the miserable life I lead."

Jorge regarded her for a long moment, then turned and called to the bartender, "Another bottle, *por favor,*" before returning his attention to her. "Tell me what happened."

"Why do you care?"

"I am your friend," he said. "How could I not care?"

Ramona looked up in surprise. She expected to see laughter in his eyes, but there was only concern.

"You mean that, don't you?" she said.

"Of course. I have always been your friend."

"Why?"

"Because you are a good person. Because you treat me as an equal, when others of your clan see me as nothing more than a cactus-grazer. Because you argue better than anyone I know. Because you're gorgeous and great in bed. Because you can drink me under the table and dance me off my feet. Because..." He smiled as her mouth hung open. "Should I go on?"

She shook her head.

"So tell me what happened," he said.

Ramona hesitated, not knowing where to begin.

"I'm just really messed up," she finally said.

Jorge reached across the table and laid his hand on hers. Ramona looked down at their hands. She could feel tears brimming in her eyes. It was stupid how such a small gesture could mean so much. But it did. It meant everything.

"Rosa told me to go find my own story," she said, "but that I'm not going to know much happiness. You know, that my future's going to be bleak. Like...like my whole life's already has been, I guess."

"Oh, what does Rosa know."

"You didn't see her. She's all beatific and gentle, but underneath she's like the mountains. Strong. Unmoving. And she *knows*. I could see it in her eyes."

"*Sí*. She can seem formidable, and that — "

"Formidable. That's the perfect word to describe her. She's just so..." Ramona's voice trailed off.

"Wait a minute," she said. "*You've* met her, too, haven't you?"

"I did. It was a long time ago now. I was unhappy, just like you, but for different reasons."

"I've never known you to be unhappy."

Jorge shrugged. "I thought I should be smarter than I am. I thought with this gift of life I had been given, I should be making great and grand changes. But I didn't. I couldn't."

"So...what happened?"

"Rosa came to me in my darkness. She showed me how what is important is to do what one can. That it is the striving that is as important as the goal." He smiled. "And she told me that I should consider offering others the same kindness and decency that I would like to receive from them."

"Yeah, she told me pretty much the same thing."

"I don't find it so hard," Jorge said.

He gave her hand a squeeze. Ramona turned her own hand so that their palms lay against each other.

"I can see how that would work," she said.

The bartender brought a second glass and the bottle Jorge had ordered over to their table. Jorge pulled some money from his pocket and handed it over, including a generous tip.

"*Graçias, señor.*"

"*De nada.*"

He poured them each a glass.

"I should do something," Ramona said. "About this mess I made for Changing Dog and Corn Hair."

Jorge shook his head. "I think you should do what Rosa told you and make your own story. And prove her wrong — make it a happy one."

"But this mess I've left — "

"Would any of them listen to you?"

Ramona gave a slow shake of her head.

"Then let it go," he said. "Sometimes the best thing you can do is to allow events to take their own course. I know it feels wrong, but if they don't trust you, there is too much chance that you will only make it worse."

"You're not stupid."

"<Flatterer.>"

When he lifted his glass, she raised her own and they clinked rims.

"<To you,>" she said.

"<No, Ramona. To us. Always on the outside, looking in.>"

She smiled.

"<To us,>" she agreed.

Alice

Alice and Jim walked side by side into the medicine wheel, stopping when they reached the center where Corina stood. The coyote woman neither spoke nor acknowledged their presence. A hush fell over the forest as she watched them approach, as though the canyon itself was curious about what she might say or do.

The quiet made Alice more nervous than she was already feeling. She couldn't hear the pinyon jays anymore. She couldn't hear the breeze in the trees overhead, either. All she could hear was the quickening rhythm of her own heartbeat, the blood drumming hard in her temples.

"I wasn't sure you'd be here," Jim said.

"I come here all the time," Corina told him. "I like this place, always have. Just like you."

"Like me?"

"I've seen you here a hundred times."

"Well, you're one up on me. I never noticed you."

She shrugged. "So why are you here? It's early yet."

"I know," Jim said. "I just want to get this over with."

How could he be so calm? Alice wondered as she listened to them talk. She stood shivering beside him and it was taking all she had not to simply bolt into the forest. Maybe it was the canid in him — bolder by nature, especially compared to the jackalope's heart that still beat deep in the chest of this five-fingered being she appeared to be. Inside her, all her learning and confidence had fled and she was only the jackalope once more, mesmerized into immobility by the nearness of these two canids. Coyote and red dog.

"So what happens now?" Jim asked when Corina made no response.

Corina raised an eyebrow.

"You know and I know," he went on. "No one's going to fall in love with me without question — especially not between now and the week or so we've got left until the hundred years are up."

"You're not interested in these last few days you have left to you?"

Jim shook his head. "But I have a favor to ask."

"Another favor?"

"Well, I'm thinking it's the first, though I guess that depends on how you look at what you did to us. See, I don't remember asking for anything that other time we met, so for me this would be the first."

Alice saw humor flicker in Corina's eyes. She didn't know if that was a good sign or a bad one, but it made her pulse quicken still more.

"What's the favor?" Corina asked.

"Let Alice go."

Alice started to protest, but Jim held up a hand.

"Let me finish," he told her, then turned back to Corina. "She did her part. She found a true love and she did like you wanted — she always supported me and tried to nudge me along the ways that would enlarge my spirit."

"And you didn't?"

Jim gave her a humorless smile. "Well, I sure as hell didn't find any true love. As for the rest..." He shrugged. "Beats me. I just know that Alice shouldn't have to suffer when I'm the one who messed up. I don't care what it takes, what you need from me. Whatever you want in exchange for doing this, you've got it."

"That's an easy request to fulfill," Corina told him. "And I need nothing more from you to allow it to happen."

Alice wasn't sure she'd heard right. But as soon as she managed to process Corina's words she found the courage that had eluded her from the moment they'd first seen the coyote woman waiting for them in the medicine wheel.

"No," she said. "That's not fair. Jim never — "

"The hell it isn't," Jim broke in. "You've got a deal, Corina."

"Wait," Corina said. "Let me hear what Alice has to say."

"Come on," Jim said to Alice. "Don't mess this up. Take the gift. Go back to Thomas and live the life you're supposed to live."

Alice didn't know which was worse: seeing Jim begging for a favor on her account, or how ready one part of her was to accept it and be gone.

"I can't," she said.

"Please, Alice. Let me do this one good thing in my life. I'd like to go out knowing that if you ever think of me in the days to come, you'll remember that at least I gave you this."

But Alice continued to shake her head.

"He has a point," Corina said.

"No, he doesn't. He's never had much of anything, and for sure he's never had love until this past week. I've at least had my years with Thomas. If anybody's going to get to keep their gift, it should be him."

"But he says he wants to do this one good thing," Corina said. "Surely you don't want to deny him that?"

Alice glared at Jim before returning her attention to the coyote woman.

"That's bullshit," she said. "Ask Search & Rescue how many people he's tracked down in the wilds and brought back. Or all the other people he's helped over the years — humans and cousins. He's always there with gas or some mechanical know-how for a broken-down vehicle. He's mended fences and buildings, freed cousins from traps, distracted hunters at the risk of his own hide. He might not have actively searched out spiritual growth, but his spirit walks tall all the same."

Corina smiled.

"If you want to know the truth," she said, "you've both more than met the expectations I had for you when I stopped a red dog from making a meal out of one of his cousins. So why don't you both go home and live out the rest of your lives in what peace you can find. All I ask is that you remember how you were given a gift, and pass it on, when and where you can."

For a long moment, Alice couldn't speak. But finally she cleared her throat.

"Really?" she asked. "It's over — just like that — and we can go?"

Corina nodded.

Jim studied the coyote woman, head cocked to one side. "You were never going to change us back, were you?"

Corina shrugged. "Probably not. Not unless you'd brought more hurt into the world than the good you've done."

"Then why lay it out for us the way you did? Why make such a big production of this bargain and the hundred years and all?"

His voice was rising and Alice put a hand on his arm, trying to calm him down. They had everything they could hope for, she wanted to tell him. Don't truly make a mess of it now.

But Corina didn't appear to take offense.

"Because if I've learned anything over the years," she said, "it's that the gift freely given is never appreciated so much as the one that comes with a price attached to it." She smiled. "Even if that price is only words that can be blown away by the wind."

Alice felt the muscles of Jim's arms tense, but before she could say anything, he shook his head and laughed.

"Yeah, well, you did a good job of it," he said.

Corina shrugged. "It's the rare individual who will understand the gift for what it is when it's offered freely. Rarer still is the one who will come to me and ask. So I'm forced to be devious."

Jim got out his tobacco and rolled cigarettes, handing them round to Corina and Alice, keeping the last for himself. When they lit up, the smoke from their cigarettes rose up from the medicine wheel, mingling in the still air.

"Why do you do it?" Alice asked the coyote woman.

"I'm like my brother Cody. I want to fix the world, just like he does, only I've never made the grand gestures the way he used to. Working on that kind of scale means big-time repercussions if you screw up. And history seems to prove that the bigger the scale, the more chance there is that something *will* screw up. So I approach it one being at a time — waking the sleeping potential in them and putting them on the medicine road. Hoping they'll come to care for this world as much as I do and try to make it a better place."

"That's a long haul," Jim said.

"I'm in it for the long haul."

He nodded. "But you could probably make a bigger difference — even on an individual basis — if you targeted people with more influence, like, say, the CEOs of the power and mining companies."

"I've tried," she said, "but there's usually not enough spirit in them for me to work with."

"No surprise there, I guess."

"So when you chose us," Alice began, "how did you know we'd work out?"

"I didn't."

Corina lifted her head suddenly, gaze tracking something beyond the wheel in which they stood, perhaps beyond this world itself. Alice and Jim tried to follow the coyote woman's gaze, then looked at each other, neither of them able to see what had distracted her.

"I have to go," Corina said. She laid a hand on each of their heads, like a benediction. "Walk tall and take care of each other."

Before they could reply, she stepped away into *el entre*. A moment later, they heard the distant sound of a motorcycle starting up.

Alice and Jim stood looking at each other. Alice could hear the jays again, the wind in the trees overhead. She sat down on one of the low stone walls that joined to form a cross inside the medicine wheel.

"Well, that was...strange," she said.

Jim nodded and sat down beside her. He took out his tobacco and rolled another cigarette. When he offered it to her, Alice shook her head.

"I almost feel let down," he said after he'd gotten it lit.

"You can't be serious."

"Not really. It's just...we've lived with this hanging over our lives for a hundred years. I feel a little off-balance with it gone."

"I suppose." Alice shook her head. "I was so scared when we first walked up to her."

"Me, too."

"You? You seemed so calm, the way you were just talking like we'd run into her on some street corner."

"Trust me," Jim said. "I was shivering inside."

Alice lifted her arms above her head and stretched, then turned and smiled at her companion.

"I feel so...free," she said.

Jim nodded, but he didn't speak. He just took another drag from his cigarette and looked out past the medicine wheel, into the forest.

"You don't?" Alice asked.

He shrugged. "What I feel is lost. I thought I could end this empty feeling in my chest and just go back to being some old desert dog, scrabbling out a living in the wilds. Instead, Corina's laid on me the responsibility of going on in the world like I did before, except this time my heart's in pieces."

"Oh, Jim."

She laid a hand on his arm, horrified at herself for having forgotten the trauma that had driven him here to meet Corina earlier than necessary.

He gave her a faint smile that held no humor. "Yeah, I know. It bites, but what can you do? You can't make people care for you."

"But now you've got the time — "

"To what? To try and win her back?"

Alice nodded.

He shook his head. Taking a last drag from his cigarette, he dropped it in the dirt and ground it out. He pocketed the butt and stood up.

"We should go back," he said. "Get the logistics of breaking up dealt with. You don't mind driving them back to Tucson, do you?"

"No, but — "

But she was talking to his back. Scrambling to her feet, she joined him just as he stepped into *el entre*.

Laurel

I knew who I needed to see. The trouble was, I didn't know where to find her. The first and only time I'd met Corina had been at the Hole, the club where we'd played when we first got to Tucson. I knew nothing about her except that she was this coyote woman who could wake things in people. Or at least she'd made it so that a red dog and a jackalope could walk like — how had Alice put it? — five-fingered beings. And therefore, one supposed, she could also wake the animal blood in five-fingered beings. At least, I hoped she could. And would.

But I didn't know where she lived. I didn't even know her last name.

I'd started from our room, full of confidence and purpose, but stopped now in the lobby, realizing I didn't have a clue where to go.

I saw the desk clerk looking at me, so I smiled and gave him a wave, then went outside to the parking lot.

"Corina, Corina," I sang softly to myself. "Where do I find you?"

I'd start at the Hole, I decided. Maybe someone there would be able to help me. But before I could go back inside to call myself a cab, I heard the deep, throaty roar of a motorcycle engine. Turning in the direction of the sound, I saw that the machine was an old Indian — I recognized it because one of Adie's old boyfriends had one and was forever going on about its virtues. And then I recognized the rider. I didn't need to see her face. Who else wore all that black with the turquoise jewelry?

She rolled up to where I was standing and put a foot on the ground to keep the bike steady, but left the engine idling.

"Okay, this is weird," I said. "I was just thinking about you."

"And singing my name."

I blinked in surprise. "How could you *possibly* have heard that?"

"The same way I know why you wanted to see me."

This was a little creepy.

"You mean you can read my mind?" I asked.

She shook her head. "But I can read your intent. Think of it as a radio and I've sort of had you on a pre-set channel."

"Ohh-kay..."

"Because I like you," she said. "You're interesting."

I can't remember anybody ever saying that to me before.

"So can you do it?" I asked. "Wake this animal spirit thing in me?"

She smiled. "First I need you to tell me why you want it."

"It's for my sister..."

"You want to wake the blood in *her?*"

I shook my head. "No, I think people have to make that decision for themselves."

Something changed in those dark eyes of hers, there and gone again, too quick for me to read. But I thought it might have been approval.

"I want it woken in me," I went on, "so that she can see that it's not such a bad thing."

"How do you know it isn't?"

"I've talked to Alice."

"Mmm."

"So will you help me?"

She shook her head. "Not until you tell me why you really want it."

"I..."

I just did, I was about to say, but I knew it wasn't true, so I left those words unsaid.

"I love my family," I said, instead. "I love them all, especially Bess. But I've always carried this uncertainty around inside me, this idea that there was something more, but I'm just not connecting to it. Talking to Alice, being here, in the desert...I think this is the piece I'm missing. So I guess what I'm looking for is a closer connection and having the animal spirit in me woken seems like the best way to do that."

Corina smiled. "Well...when you put it like that, yes, I can certainly help you. Get on."

"On your bike?"

"Unless you want to change into a deer right here in the parking lot in front of whomever might be looking."

"No, of course not."

"Hold on," she said when I'd gotten on.

I grabbed hold of her as she peeled out of the lot, darting into some oncoming traffic. I closed my eyes and wrapped my arms around her waist, waiting for the impact that never came. When I opened my eyes again, she'd made a right turn, then took another one into an alleyway, going way too fast so far as I was concerned. I could see the traffic going by at the far end of the alley, but before we reached it, everything shimmered like it had back under Cathedral Rock and I knew where we were.

It was that between place that Alice had some Spanish name for that I couldn't remember. The place between our world and the spirit world.

Corina slowed the Indian to a stop and cut the engine. When she did, the silence seemed to echo in my head. I felt a little dizzy and I wasn't sure if it was from crossing over, or the wild ride on Corina's bike.

I got off the bike and Corina put it on its kickstand.

I did a slow 360 degrees, taking in the view all around. I recognized the shapes of the mountains, if nothing else. It was all desert, running right up into the foothills, a forest of saguaro and cacti and shrubs.

"This...this is still Tucson, isn't it?" I said.

"Yes and no. It's where Tucson is in the spiritlands."

"This isn't the between place?"

She shook her head.

"It's..."

I was going to say overwhelming, but it wasn't really. It was intense, the air so clean and fresh, the landscape...everything...so *present*.

"It's beautiful," I said.

"It is, isn't it."

"And I don't even feel woozy — like I did when I crossed over with Alice. Well, I did for a moment, but it went right away."

"Some people adjust quicker than others. Maybe you're a fast learner."

"I guess. So..."

I looked around. We were certainly alone here. No one was going to see me change into an animal. No, not just an animal. A red deer. I felt like I was about to go on stage for some big gig, a little nervous, a lot of anticipation.

"How does it work?" I asked.

She stepped up to me. "Just like this."

She put a hand on the back of my head, then leaned in and kissed me, her other hand circling around to the small of my back and drawing me in close to her.

It's funny. I would have thought kissing another woman would have been...I don't know. Softer, I guess. And her lips *were* soft. But the rest of her was muscle, firm and strong — except for the disconcerting press of her breasts against mine.

I wasn't sure what to do. I suppose I thought that this was how she was going to wake the animal spirit in me. So I tried to relax with it, but then her tongue darted into my mouth and I pulled back.

She let me go and smiled. "Not your style?"

"I...it's just...well, you know...if this is how you do it...waking the animal spirit in me and everything..."

Her smile deepened.

"I was waking a different kind of animal spirit," she said, "and it looks like it was only waking in me."

"So this isn't how...you know...?"

"No. Remember how you were wondering if I was hitting on you that night in the Hole?"

"How'd you know that?"

"The same way you figured I might be hitting on you."

"Oh."

"And I was."

"Look, I'm sorry, but I'm not...being with a woman like that just doesn't work for me. It's not who I am."

"You're lucky to be so sure of who you are at such a young age."

It was hard to tell if she was making fun of me or what. Actually, it was hard to get any kind of a reading from her. She just stood there, so relaxed and comfortable in herself — obviously not feeling any of the awkwardness I did. For my part, I was more than ready to move on to the real reason we were supposed to have come here, but I found myself asking about something else instead.

"This thing about you being attracted to me," I said. "Is it something I'm doing?"

Corina just looked at me.

"It's just that it's been happening to me a lot lately — women hitting on me, I mean — and I was wondering why it was."

"Have you looked in a mirror lately?"

"I look exactly the same as Bess, but women aren't hitting on her."

"And it bothers you?"

"No. Yes. I don't know. It's just weird. I feel like ever since we started this last tour, I've become a babe-magnet."

Corina smiled. "You think I'm a babe?"

"Have *you* looked in a mirror lately?"

"I just wanted to hear you say it. And," she added before I could go on, "I don't know what it is about you and Bess. Or at least, I can't say what it is for anyone else. My being attracted to you seems to work on some kind of intuitive, maybe chemical level. Yes, you look the same as your sister. You're both pretty and smart and talented. But you make my heart go pitter-pat and she doesn't."

I gave her a slow nod. "So how did you know that you were..."

"Bi?"

"You're bi?"

"Mmhmm. Being attracted to men was obvious, considering the company I keep. Canids are always interested in sex. Being attracted to women as well was just a pleasant surprise."

"Oh. And I guess your bringing me here — "

"Was full of all sorts of ulterior motives, like getting you into my bed."

"I was going to say, was it to see if I'd be a pleasant surprise, too, which is pretty much the same thing."

"Pretty much."

Neither of us said anything for a long moment. I wished I didn't feel so awkward. It was so beautiful here, but I couldn't put her being attracted to me out of my head. Before it had been kind of, you know, the way a guy checks you out, but now there was a wistfulness in the way she looked at me that made me feel sad for her. Because I did like her — if not in the way she might have preferred — and that made me wish I could get past the nervousness I was feeling that she'd hit on me again. I was sure she wouldn't, but it was there all the same. I just wanted to be comfortable around her.

I sighed. When she turned to me and raised her eyebrows, I looked for something to say.

"So," I said. "I guess you can't really..."

"Wake the red deer in you?"

I nodded.

"Of course, I can. I can and I will."

She reached a hand towards me, this time laying it on the top of my head. I wasn't sure what I was supposed to feel, what the wakening would be like. What happened was I got a shiver, deep in my chest, that spread out in waves throughout me.

Do you see this? she said. *How it all connects?*

Her voice was in my head somehow, like she was in here with me, and I was able to see the whole inside of myself, gaining an awareness of how all the tiny little molecules that made me who I am fit together and worked. And how they could be adjusted to match the faint blueprint of another shape that was hidden in the memory of my genes.

The way to make the shift was so easy, but I can't explain exactly how it worked. I guess the simplest way to describe it is that it was like being able to throw a switch I'd never known was there before.

And then...and then...

This is the hardest to try to explain. I was still me, with everything I knew and felt and that made me who I am, but at the same time I wasn't me anymore. A whole wave of unfamiliar sensations and knowledge swept over me, lying like gauze upon the me I'd always been. I was standing on four trembling legs. My sense of smell and hearing and sight multiplied a hundredfold. I took a wobbly step, but the motion made me lose my balance, and then down I went.

"Oh, dear," Corina said.

She took a step towards me and I panicked at her approach, shifting back to my human shape, which left me sprawled on the ground. And naked. But I have to say this for Corina. Where she could have stood there gawking at me, instead, she moved her hands in the air above where I was lying and I had my clothes again. Well, they were pretty much my clothes. She did make a few adjustments — the neckline on my blouse was a lot lower than it had been before and the jeans were a lot tighter — but hey, at least I was wearing something, even if the something was sexier than what I had started out in.

"You have to think about clothes," she said as she helped me to my feet. "When you shift to your animal shape, their molecules are absorbed by your surroundings. When you shift back again, you have to remember to think of what you want to be wearing so that you don't show up like you just did — buck naked."

She went on to explain how exactly it was done.

"So I don't have to come back wearing what I was when I first shifted?" I asked.

Corina shook her head. "You can be wearing anything you like. And it doesn't work just when you're shifting. You can do it any time, which let me tell you, is a huge savings on your wardrobe budget."

She moved her hands through the air around herself, starting with her shoulders and going down to her feet. I shouldn't have been surprised anymore, but I couldn't help blinking when suddenly she was standing there in heels and a little black cocktail dress, still wearing her turquoise jewelry, but it was toned down to no more than a ring, a pendant, and some earrings.

"See?" she said.

She repeated the motion with her hands and she was back to the black jeans and T-shirt she'd been wearing before, a half-dozen bracelets jingling on either wrist.

"Now you try it," she said.

So I did what she'd shown me, adjusting the molecules around myself and, just for the fun of it, picturing the kinds of clothes that my younger sisters liked. And then there I was, standing in front of Corina in baggy cargo pants and a midriff baring white T-shirt.

"Oh, this is going to be a nightmare," I said.

"I thought you liked clothes. At least that's the way it seems from the care you take in dressing yourself."

"I do. I love them. And now it's going to take me hours longer trying to decide what to wear. I mean, if you have access to *anything...*"

She laughed. "On the plus side, you won't need much in the way of luggage anymore."

"This is too cool," I said as I changed my look back to the jeans and top I'd had on when we first got here.

"You should practice your shift to animal some more," Corina told me.

"It was so weird," I said. "I completely forgot how to *walk.*"

"That's because you're keeping too tight a grip on also being human. You have to sink a little deeper into the animal shape — let its instincts take over the basics of using your new body. But you also have to be careful not to go too deep, especially in the first little while. It's easy, and seductive, to just let yourself go."

"What happens then?"

"You might stay the deer and never come back."

"Oh."

I didn't like the sound of that.

"Don't look so worried," she said. "Just remember: everything in moderation."

"I guess."

"So try it for a little longer. Shift to the deer and go for a run."

"Will you come with me?"

She shook her head. "I don't think that's such a good idea. The woman you are is feeling a little skittish around me — "

I started to protest, but she cut me off.

"We both know it's true," she said. "It's part of what made you panic, right after you fell. And the deer you can become will naturally want to avoid the coyote in me. It'll be different when you have more control, but right now it's all instinct, and instinct's telling both parts of you that I could be dangerous."

"And are you?" I couldn't help asking.

"Not to you."

I believed her, I don't know why. I guess it was because the more I got to know her, the more I liked her — though still not in the way she was hoping I would — and when you like somebody, you tend to give them some slack. Or maybe for all my worldly experience as a traveling musician over the past couple of years, in my heart, I still was just the naïve hillbilly girl that Bess and I had both been when we first left Tyson County to make a go of it on our own.

"Do you think we could be friends?" I said.

She smiled. "I was hoping we already were."

"I meant just friends."

"I know you did. Now go practice."

So I did.

The shift was easy and this time I managed to keep my balance, standing there on my four trembling legs, but walking was still awkward. I took a couple of faltering steps, then glanced over at Corina. She looked very strange from this new perspective of mine and smelled...worrisome.

My deer's heart beat a little quicker, sensing the predator in her.

"Easy now," Corina said, her voice pitched low and comforting. "No one's going to harm you here."

I tried to say, I know that, but it came out as a kind of bleat.

Corina smiled. "Remember what I said. Sink a little lower into the shape — let the deer's natural instincts guide you."

I knew that, too, but I was afraid of losing myself the way she'd said I might if I wasn't careful.

So just be careful, I told myself.

I let myself sink a little more into the deer shape and a funny thing happened. It was like lowering myself into a warm bath — comfortable and welcoming. The deer shape embraced me. It knew me. It *was* me.

"Careful," Corina said. "You're sinking too far."

But I just made a happy sound, prancing in place, hooves clicking on the stones. I could never sink too far into this shape. That was like saying you were being too much yourself.

"Laurel."

I looked at the woman, not quite sure who she was. When she took a step towards me, I backed quickly away, nervous again. There was a strong scent of coyote about her, which was puzzling, because she was obviously a five-fingered being, not a hunter. Except...except the five-fingered beings hunted, too...

When she took another step, I turned and bolted.

I heard her cry after me, but that only made me laugh.

My legs were strong and I ran fast, fast, fast — faster than any five-fingered being could. She would never catch me.

Alice

Alice knew there was something wrong as soon as they got back to the motel's parking lot, but she couldn't put her finger on what it was until Jim spoke.

"Aw, no," he said. "I can't believe they took my truck."

He was right. That old rusted '57 Ford of his was nowhere to be seen. There was only her Forester, still parked where she'd left it after they'd gotten back from the gig last night.

Jim walked over to the empty spot beside her car and sighed.

"I didn't take her for a spiteful woman," he said.

"I'm sure they just borrowed it to get back to Tucson."

"Right."

"Well, how else were they supposed to get back?"

"They didn't have to go back with me. You could have given them a lift."

Alice shook her head. "From what you told me about last night, I don't think I'm exactly in Bess's good books, either."

"I suppose. But to take my truck..."

Alice shook her head and headed for the stairs. Jim hesitated for a moment, then went into the room he'd shared with Bess to get his own things. They met up back beside the Forester.

"See," Alice said, handing over the note that Laurel had written to her. "They're going to leave it in the Hotel Congress parking lot for you. Do you want a ride back, or are you going by *el entre?*"

"I'll take the lift, thanks. I need time to think."

And maybe to not be alone just now, Alice thought.

"When we pick up your truck in Tucson," Alice began as she pulled out of the parking lot.

"If it's there to be picked up."

"*When* we pick up your truck," she repeated, "you should come back to the house with me."

Jim shook his head. "No offense, but I'm not exactly in the mood for socializing."

"You don't have to. You can sit in a corner and frown at us and we won't say a thing. But you shouldn't be alone right now."

"Come on, Alice. I'm not going to kill myself."

"I know. But I still think you shouldn't be alone. And besides, I could use your help trying to convince Thomas to start spending some time in *el entre.*"

Jim laughed, but there was no humor in the sound. "Yeah, I'm real good at talking to people. Just think of how well it went last night with Bess."

"Well, you are, actually. I think there were some other issues at work last night."

"What's that supposed to mean?"

"I don't mean you. I mean Bess. I don't think her last encounter with the otherworld left a very good impression."

"It doesn't seem to have bothered Laurel."

Alice smiled. "Yes, and they're exactly the same, aren't they?"

"Okay. Point taken. But it doesn't solve anything."

"Some things we can't solve," Alice said. "We just have to get through them. But if you want my opinion — "

"Which you're so rarely willing to share."

She was ready to jab him with her elbow, but a glance in his direction showed that the ghost of a smile was actually playing on his lips.

"You can't just leave it like this," she said. "You have to do something. Talk to her. Win her back."

"That's not going to happen. You weren't there. You didn't — "

"See her face. I know. You already told me that. But you caught her off guard and I'm sure things were said in the heat of the moment that neither of you really meant. You should talk to her again — before they leave town."

When he didn't reply, she looked over at him.

"You do want her back, don't you?" she asked.

"I'd give anything to have her back," Jim said. "Except for your happiness."

Alice was ready with a sarcastic reply of her own, except she realized that he really meant it.

"I don't think it'll come to that," she said instead.

They drove a few miles in silence, neither taking as much pleasure from the landscape as they normally would.

"So why do you want Thomas to spend more time in *el entre?*" Jim asked.

Alice shrugged. "I just don't want to lose him. He's sixty-two now. We used to go on three-or-four-day camping trips and daylong hikes — really roughing it. But he can't do it anymore because even with the exercising he does, he doesn't have the same stamina. He's getting old."

"*El entre* isn't going to make him young again."

"I know. But spending some time there will slow the aging process and give him more vitality. I know he misses going out with me as much as I miss his company."

"But he's afraid of being changed."

Alice nodded.

"That's becoming a familiar litany," Jim said.

"You said you didn't offer to wake Bess's animal blood."

"I didn't. But she's just as afraid of magic and shapeshifting as Thomas is. More, I guess. Thomas didn't turn from you when he found out."

Alice smiled. "I don't think he really believes it. I mean he's seen me with antlers and rabbit ears, and he knows the whole story of Corina and all, but it doesn't seem to stick with him."

"I wish that would happen with Bess."

"Do you really?"

Jim shook his head. "No. Not really."

It was another five minutes or so before Jim spoke up again.

"When you talk to Thomas about the otherworld," he asked, "do you emphasize the pluses for him?"

"Of course."

"So maybe you're approaching this from the wrong direction. Maybe you should try asking him to do it for you, instead. If he cares half as much for you as I do — and we both know he probably cares twice as much — he'll do it."

Alice stared at the road.

"I never thought of that," she said finally.

Red Deer Woman

Bess

I WASN'T TOO worried when I first woke in the hotel room to find myself alone. Laurel wouldn't have wanted to disturb me, so she was probably downstairs in the lobby or café, or had gone out for a little sightseeing. For one thing, there were all those stores over on Fourth Avenue that we'd only got to look at through their windows the other night. But an uneasiness crept over me as I got out of the bed. I saw that her fiddle was still stacked with the rest of our gear along the wall by the door. Looking around, I didn't see a note, but that wasn't giving me this funny feeling inside. What bothered me was that I couldn't *feel* her like I always did.

It was like that awful moment yesterday when she'd told me she'd had vertigo, but then admitted later that what had really happened was that she'd stepped into fairyland with Alice.

She couldn't — she *wouldn't* — have done that again. I just couldn't imagine it. Not without telling me first.

But why couldn't I *feel* her?

I hated to think that it might have something to do with her accepting Jim and Alice and magic and everything, and my not being able to. That something like that could have broken the bond between us.

It's funny how you can be so up one day and then the next, everything's crap. I knew a lot of it was perspective, but between what had happened with Jim yesterday, and now this sense of somehow having lost my connection to Laurel, I was operating at way low ebb and I didn't have any sense of perspective. How could I? It was all happening right now.

I pulled back the covers and only managed to make it to the edge of the bed where I sat and stared at the wall. I'd slept way deeper than I thought I would, and for much longer, but it didn't appear to have done me any good. Truth was, I was exhausted. And all I had to do was think of Jim and everything got tight inside me again and my vision blurred. I felt like calling Adie — who had way more experience with boys — to ask her how long this feeling would last, but she'd want to know everything and what would I tell her? She'd experienced fairyland along with the rest of us, but she was also the least interested in talking about it.

I sighed and had a shower, then wiped the fog from the mirror and stared at my reflection for awhile, trying to decide if the puffiness around my eyes had gone down enough for me to venture downstairs.

There was nothing I could do about what had happened with Jim, but I couldn't stand feeling this way about Laurel.

She wasn't in the lobby or the café. Or outside, where it was already starting to get dark again. I saw that Jim's pickup was gone from the overflow parking lot where Laurel said she'd left it.

Even with my worry for Laurel, I knew a small pang of disappointment that he hadn't tried to see me. Okay, so I told him I never wanted to see him again, but that doesn't mean he couldn't have *tried*.

This whole jangle of emotions started whirling around in my head. Wanting to see him. Knowing there was no point — how could he change what he was? Remembering how Laurel thought I was acting like Buck and the way he felt about gays. Remembering how *right* all the time with Jim had felt. Remembering how he'd turned into a dog...

That memory shut everything else down.

Except for the sadness. I didn't feel like I'd ever lose the sadness.

When I went back into the lobby, I walked up to the desk. The clerk smiled at me and I tried to remember what it felt like to smile. Couldn't.

"Wow," he said. "You two really are identical, aren't you?"

"Pretty much. Have you seen my sister Laurel today?"

"Yeah, she was down here again a little while after you guys checked in earlier."

"She didn't say where she was going, did she?"

He shook his head. "She went off with a woman riding a beautifully reconditioned Indian."

I gave him a blank look.

"It's a kind of motorcycle," he explained.

"Oh. Right."

Then I realized what he'd said. Laurel had gone off with a woman? The only one I could think of was Alice.

"Was she Native American — but with blonde hair?" I asked. "And not very tall?"

"No. I mean, she was an Indian, but she was tall and slinky with long black hair. And that bike."

He grinned in appreciation, but then got a concerned look. I guess I'd gone all pale or something.

"Hey, are you okay?" he asked.

I nodded. "I'm just coming down with some kind of bug. I think I'll go back to our room."

But when I reached the top of the stairs, out of his sight, I sat down, trying to make sense of this. From the desk clerk's description, Laurel had gone off with Corina. But why would she do that? All Laurel had done since Corina had talked to her back at the Hole was complain about Corina hitting on her.

And where would they have gone?

We — or at least I — didn't know anything about her except that she was this scary Coyote Woman who could change animals into people and...maybe vice versa?

When the realization came to me, I didn't even want to think about it. But taking in the things Laurel had been saying on the drive back to Tucson and her sympathies for Alice and Jim, it made an awful kind of sense. And of course, she wouldn't talk to me first, because she knew exactly how I'd feel about it.

I had to stop her. Though maybe I was already too late. Maybe this was the reason I couldn't *feel* her anymore. It wasn't because she'd disappeared from the world. It was because she'd become something else.

I scrambled to my feet and hurried back to the room where I went through Laurel's purse looking for the phone number I knew had to be in there. When I found it, I sat down on the bed and made the call. It rang enough times that I thought it was going to go to an answering machine but then someone picked up.

"Hello?"

I took a breath. I didn't want to talk to Alice. For all I knew, she was a part of this craziness that had Laurel going off with Corina to get turned into some kind of animal.

But I didn't have any choice. There was no one else I knew that I could talk to.

"It's Bess," I said.

There was a moment's silence, then, "How are you doing?" Alice asked. Her voice was warm and sympathetic.

How was I doing? Awful. Horrible. Terrible.

"I'm calling about Laurel," I said. "She's gone off somewhere with Corina and I think she's about to do something stupid."

No, that was the wrong thing to say. That was like saying Alice was stupid. But it was too late to take it back.

"Where are you?" Alice asked.

"At the Hotel Congress."

"Stay there," she said. "We'll be right over."

Then she hung up.

I stared at the phone receiver.

What did she mean by "we"?

But I knew.

God, I wasn't ready for any of this.

555

It took them about half an hour to get to the hotel. I'd gone down to the café for a coffee and something to eat while I waited. I hadn't been able to actually eat more than a few bites from my sandwich, but I was on my second coffee when I saw Jim's pickup pull into the parking lot.

It's weird. The first thing I felt when I saw him get out of the truck was this happy little jump in my heart. Like we were still a couple. His gaze settled on me and even after everything, those violet eyes of his could still do it for me. But then my memories of last night swelled up and that moment of false happiness got smothered.

I didn't know if I could do this. It was so hard seeing him again.

This isn't about you, I told myself. This is about Laurel. You can do this.

I got up and left some money on the table, then went out to talk to them.

It wasn't much consolation, but meeting like this seemed just as hard on Jim. I could tell that he wanted to look at me, made himself not do it — a whole world of emotion warring in his eyes. Sadness, hope, need, hopelessness. All the things that were going around in my own head.

I don't know what would have happened if it had just been the two of us, but Alice was there, too. She immediately came up to me and gave me a hug. And even though I knew she was really some kind of cross between a hare and a deer, I was grateful for that contact and hugged her back.

"This has got to be so hard on you," she said.

I almost broke down and cried, right there and then. Somehow I managed to hold it all in and tell them what I knew.

"You were the only ones I could think of," I said, finishing up. "When I couldn't feel her anymore in...in this world, and then the desk clerk told me she'd gone off with Corina..."

"So that's what distracted her," Jim said.

"Distracted her? What are you talking about?"

Alice filled me in on what had happened at the medicine wheel, after the two of them had left the motel together.

After the big fight Jim and I'd had...

A little of that anger was back now, but it was directed at — oh, I don't know. Jim, a little. Corina, for sure. The world in general, that everything could be so messed up and unfair.

"So what does this mean?" I asked. "Is Laurel supposed to be taking my place in this...in whatever you guys had happening with Corina...?"

"It's not like that," Jim said. "For one thing, we're free of the curse now. Turns out there never even was one. For another, you, specifically, were never part of it."

"I know. It was just anybody who'd fall in love with you."

He shook his head. "That's not why I fell in love with you. I had a hundred years to find someone. I just didn't until I met you."

"When your time was almost up."

Jim gave Alice a pleading look.

"He's telling the truth," she said. "You were everything to him — never a means to an end."

"Whatever."

Okay that was downright mean, and I knew it, but I couldn't help myself. And I couldn't seem to make myself apologize for it either.

"It still doesn't explain what's happened to Laurel," I went on. "Did Corina take her as some kind of payment? You know, because I wasn't available?"

"It was never about that," Jim said.

"Yeah, right."

"I know you don't want to," Alice said, "but did you ever consider that this is something Laurel *wanted* to do?"

"After she was brainwashed."

I saw a look in Alice's eyes that I hadn't seen before and realized it was anger. Up until now, she'd always been so calm and peaceful that I'd never considered her as capable of being anything else.

"We're wasting time," she said. She'd kept her voice calm but the anger continued to flash in her eyes. "We have to go — "

"Where?"

"And you," she said as though I'd never interrupted, "need to wait here."

"Why?"

"Because Laurel's in a place that you don't even want to know about, never mind visit."

Nobody had to say it. We all knew she was talking about the otherworld.

I looked from one to the other. "I'm going to call the police and file a missing persons report."

"Okay," Alice said.

My gaze fixed on Jim. "And I'm going to tell them you were involved."

"Do whatever you feel you need to do," Alice said. "Meanwhile, we're going to find your sister."

And then I started to cry.

I just stood there in the parking lot with my shoulders shaking and the tears rolling down my cheeks.

Alice was the one who stepped forward and held me.

"It's okay," she said. "We'll find her. And we'll bring her back. I promise."

"I...I'm just...so scared...for her..."

I could barely talk through the tears.

"I know you are," she said. "If it's any consolation, I know for a fact that Corina would never purposely harm her."

I nodded into her shoulder and stepped back. Sniffling. I wiped my eyes on my sleeve. Someone held something out to me and I realized it was Jim. He'd gotten a paper towel from the pickup. I nodded my thanks to him and blew my nose in it, then looked at the two of them.

"I'm coming with you," I said.

They both shook their heads.

"That's not such a good idea," Alice said.

"I've been there before, you know. Not here, but back home. In Tyson County. We...Laurel and Sarah Jane and I...we faced down a whole army of bee fairies."

"I'm not saying you're not brave," Alice said. "It's just...well, you've got these issues..."

"Let her come," Jim said.

We both looked at him.

"It's her sister," he said. "Even if it scared me as much as it does Bess, I'd do it if it were either of you. You'd do it if it were Thomas."

Alice didn't say anything for a moment, but then she nodded her head.

"Come on," she said.

She led the way across Toole Avenue to the overflow parking lot, guiding us in among the cars, away from the lights of the hotel and street to where it was darker. Both she and Jim looked around.

"I think we're okay," he said. "No one's paying attention."

"Take my hand," Alice said.

I did.

And the next thing I knew I was hit with a wave of vertigo and we were somewhere else.

No, that's not true, I realized. We were in the same place, only it was in the otherworld. The city was gone, but the landscape remained unchanged. Except it was lit by bright moonlight instead of city lights — so bright, it cast shadows. It reminded me of that first night in the desert with Jim, before the weirdness and lies drove a wedge between us. Before Laurel disappeared.

I'd been really nervous as we crossed over, but now I was feeling too sick to my stomach to be scared. It was weird. This hadn't happened when I'd been in the Tyson County version of this place. But while I was too busy feeling nauseous to be scared, it was so quiet that when a voice did speak up, I understood the expression of almost jumping out of your skin.

"I have some ginger tea — maybe that will help her."

I turned to see Corina and her motorcycle, but no sign of Laurel. I still couldn't feel her, either.

Corina got a thermos out of the saddlebag of her motorcycle and brought it over. I was a little wary about taking anything from her, but I was also feeling too sick to my stomach to much care. If this'd help, I'd try it.

She poured some of the tea into the cup of the thermos. When she offered it to me, I downed it in one gulp.

"Give it a moment or two," she said. "Medicines always need time, even here in the spiritworld where their benefits are accelerated."

She poured me another cup of the tea and I sat down in the dirt with it, sipping it more slowly while the three of them talked. It was weird seeing Alice here — she had long rabbit ears hanging like braids along either side of her face and small antlers on her brow. Jim looked just like he always did. Corina, too. As they talked, she played the innocent, of course, claiming that Laurel had come to her, but I wasn't fooled.

Once I was feeling a little better physically, I joined the conversation. I knew this wasn't being very helpful, but I was furious that they could all just play with our lives this way.

So I looked Corina straight in the eye and said, "Here's what I need to know. How could you just turn her into...into the..."

"Despicable things that we are?" Corina finished for me.

"I didn't say that."

"No," Corina said. "You didn't have to."

She was right and I realized I didn't care that she knew it. I had more important things on my mind.

"It's just...this is my sister..."

"Who made this decision for herself. I don't wake anyone's old blood lines without their permission first. They have to *want* it."

"That's true," Alice said. "At least it was for us."

"I don't *care*. All I know is Laurel's out here somewhere in your fairyland and — "

"And the other reason she's there is because of you."

I glared at Corina. "Because of *me?* Right, like I'm supposed to believe — "

"She wanted you to see that being able to access both your human and animal natures isn't such an awful, evil thing."

"I never said..."

But my voice trailed off because that wasn't true. I felt my gaze drawn to Jim, but I couldn't look at him. I'd said a lot of harsh things to him, back in Sedona, and I couldn't pretend otherwise.

"So," Corina went on. "Before you start throwing around blame, you might want to have a look in the mirror."

"Okay," Jim said, stepping in between us. "You don't have to be so hard on her."

Considering everything, I was surprised to have him stand up for me. And then I was even more surprised at the deep sorrow I saw in Corina's face.

"You're right," she said, then turned to me. "I'm sorry. I'm just so worried for her."

The weird thing was, I believed her. She seemed to be genuinely concerned — and not because of any blame that might be laid on her.

I took a deep breath and swallowed my own confused stew of feelings. Bottom line, all that was important to me right now was Laurel.

"Where is my sister?" I asked. "If she's here, in this world, how come I can't *feel* her?"

"Because she's changed," Corina said, and went on to explain what had happened when Laurel had let herself sink into her animal shape. "I can't get near her — the coyote in me sets off alarms. I've given up trying because it's making her too skittish."

"So I couldn't, either," Jim said.

Corina shook her head.

"How about if I try?" Alice asked.

"Could you keep up with her?" Corina asked. "She's fast — faster than our local deer."

"Probably not," Alice said after a moment's consideration. "I can get up a lot of speed — but only in short bursts. Still, I could give it a try."

"And then what?" Corina said. "Would she even recognize you in your animal shape? Would the deer she is listen long enough for you to reach the human inside her that you do know?"

"But we can't not try."

"I agree," Corina said. "But right now I don't even know exactly where she is. She's somewhere over there." She gave a vague wave of her hand which took in the foothills of what were known as the Tucson Mountains back in the world we'd left behind. "And that's a lot of country. If we wait too much longer who knows how far she'll get?"

"What about me?" I said. "Isn't there anything I can do?"

Nobody said anything for a long moment.

"Not really," Corina finally said. "At least, not without compromising your principles."

"What's that supposed to mean?"

Alice and Jim still didn't speak, and Corina hesitated for another long moment.

"You're not going to like this," she told me.

As soon as she said that, I knew where this was going. I looked to Jim and Alice. Jim wouldn't look at me and Alice's gaze was full of sympathy.

"I also have to tell you," Corina went on, "that I really don't agree with this. Beings need to want this knowledge for their *own* spiritual advancement — not because they've been coerced into it by circumstance."

"Why do I even have to be a deer to do this?"

"Because as a deer, the connection the two of you have will come back. You'll be able to find her and approach her."

"Okay," I said slowly. "But you said she lost herself as a deer. What's to stop the same thing from happening to me?"

"That's why we should try to find another way to do this," Corina said.

"Except," Alice finally spoke up, "do we really have the time?"

"I don't understand why there's a time limit," I said. "Why the hurry?"

I couldn't remember the last time I'd been as full of questions as I was this evening.

"The otherworld's not one place, but many," Alice explained. "It's like a quilt, all these worlds and pieces of world laid up against each other. In some, time passes more quickly than it does here; in others, much slower."

"In other words, it's a bewildering place," Jim said.

Alice nodded. "If your sister wanders out of this world into another, our finding her becomes that much harder. And if she wanders out of that one..."

"We might never find her again," I finished.

Alice nodded.

"It's why I've left her alone," Corina said. "I was afraid that the coyote in me would chase her right out of this world."

I sighed. Now I was getting too scared for Laurel to be angry anymore. I also couldn't imagine how Laurel could have gone willingly into this. Had no one explained the dangers to her?

"How did you ever...seduce her into wanting this?" I asked Corina.

"Sadly," she said, "there was no seduction involved."

I couldn't help it. Even with all that was on my mind, that made me smile.

Corina gave me a puzzled look. "What?"

"Nothing. It's just funny. Laurel and I were joking that you were hitting on her, but I don't think either of us actually believed it."

I looked away to the mountains. They were so beautiful in the moonlight. And these tall saguaro, all around us — I could *feel* their presence as well as see them. They were like a pressure touching something inside me, instilling...I'm not sure what. Not really confidence or bravery. More that what I was about to do was the right thing, no matter how much it scared me. No matter how much I'd be changed and how then all my touchstones with the world would disappear.

"You have to do this waking thing in me," I told Corina.

She shook her head. "We can't chance losing you, too. We'll think of another way."

"Why can't Alice change into this rabbit she is and come with me? She can remind me."

"I have a better idea," Alice said.

Before anyone could ask her what it was, she took a few steps away from us and began to search for something, her gaze going up to the tops of the saguaro that grew all around us in a forest where back in our world, the city of Tucson had taken over so much of their range.

"Ah, there," she said. "I see one."

And then she made an odd, bird-like cry.

For a long moment, there was no response. Then on the top of a distant saguaro, a feathered shape stirred and lifted into the air on its wings. I thought it was an owl, but then it got closer and I realized it was one of those red-tailed hawks that we also have back home in Tyson County. Except when it dropped down from the sky, it changed into a dark-skinned, black-haired man, and that's something our hawks don't do. At least, I've never seen them do it.

That was enough to make me nervous, but he had this scary vibe at the same time. It might have had something to do with the bright moonlight, how it accentuated the strong lines of his face but left only dark shadows where his eyes should be. Or maybe it was because he had the look of a man who rarely smiled, and then it would never be frivolously. Looking at him was like looking right into a dark piece of the night and finding that it was looking back at you, considering I don't know what.

But when his gaze met Alice's, a thin smile touched his lips and warmed his features.

"<Hello, little one,>" he said. "<You keep curious company this evening.>"

I knew he wasn't speaking English, but for some reason I could understand him anyway.

"This is —" Alice began.

"Anselmo," the hawk man filled in for her.

"One of my friend Bettina's many uncles," Alice went on, then introduced us to him.

"I know of the two of you," Anselmo said to Corina and Jim, speaking a heavily accented English now. "But you," he added, looking at me. "You are far from your home."

"I'm from the other side of the country," I said. "A place called Tyson County."

He nodded. "And the red deer in you is from farther still — across the great water."

I gave my companions a confused look.

"Your deer spirit isn't indigenous to North America," Alice explained. "I believe their range is in Scotland."

"My family came from there," I said. "But that's going way back."

Corina smiled. "That deer blood of yours goes 'way back,' as well."

Anselmo turned to Alice.

"Will you be at the pueblo this weekend?" he asked. "Cipriano — my eldest — is leading the Caballeros this year."

"He means the Yaqui Easter Ceremony," Alice said, looking at us, "when they dance to keep the world safe for another year."

Corina and Jim seemed to already know what she was talking about, so I assumed she was explaining it for me.

"Thomas and I come every year," Alice said, turning back to Anselmo. "It's the least we can do to give thanks and show our respect. You should come after your gig," she added to me.

Anselmo nodded. "You can meet our deer dancer."

"Maybe," I said, not wanting to be rude, but not really able to think about anything except Laurel just now. "If we make it through the night."

Anselmo raised his eyebrows questioningly.

"We have a favor to ask of you," Alice said to him and explained how we needed to figure out a way to keep tabs on me when I was in deer form.

"I can do that," he said.

So then it was up to me.

I didn't know what it was going to feel like, when Corina woke this animal blood in me, but I sure wasn't expecting it to be so easy, or — I have to admit — in any way nice. I had pictures in my head of way too many Wolfman movies — new muscles and body shapes ripping their way through frail human flesh. There'd be pain. Red demon eyes. Howling at the moon.

But, of course, deer don't howl. And learning how to shift was like...oh, I don't know. Remembering something pleasant that you hadn't thought of in a long while. Or like lying down on a soft bed after a long day on the road. Comforting.

The deer shape embraced me and when I stood there in the moonlight on four trembling legs, I felt like I'd come home.

I was still more human than deer — in my head, at least — so I wasn't too nervous when I realized that Corina'd been right about how her own cousin blood would make me skittish. I could certainly...smell the predator in her and Jim. Coyote and wild dog. Alice was a more comfortable presence — the antelope part of her jackalope reaching out to me, I guessed. Anselmo was an enigma. I couldn't read anything from him. Not hawk, not man.

But the same wasn't true of the world around me. All my senses seemed to be stronger — especially my ability to smell and hear and see. The desert that had appeared so quiet around us was now filled with the sounds of cousins going about their business and the breeze brought me as much information about what lay upwind as you can get about the week's new releases from *Billboard*.

I remembered what Corina had said about not trying to move as a deer with too much of my human mind in control, so I sank a little deeper into the deer. My new shape continued to embrace me and I could feel myself becoming more and more deer. I didn't understand Corina's worries about my losing myself in the deer. I was the deer and the deer was me. But I also didn't understand what I was doing here with these strangers.

When the jackalope woman moved towards me, I started and took a few quick steps back without even stumbling.

"Bess," she said. "Your sister."

My sister...?

But as soon as the words settled in me, I could feel a familiar connection once more.

That's right, I realized. I have a sister. Another deer, just like me. And I knew just where she was.

"You have to find Laurel," the jackalope woman said.

But she's not lost, I wanted to say.

The words came out in a series of strange bleats that made me laugh. The laughter was more of the bleats, but different. Funnier.

"Go to her," the jackalope woman said, drawing my attention back to her. "Go to your sister."

I liked that idea. I wasn't comfortable with these beings. I wanted to be with my sister. We could run together under the moonlight. But until I reached her, I had to run alone.

I turned and sprang off, galloping full out, delighting in the drum of my hooves on the dry ground and rocks, stretching my legs, the desert air cool on my fur, the moonlight showing me the way. I don't know how long I ran, but after awhile I slowed to a trot.

I could feel the pull of my sister. Every step I took brought me closer to her.

I thought I was being followed and stopped a time or two, looking back, reading the wind. But there was no one.

I didn't think to look up.

The night was alive with cousins. I startled a herd of javalinas, feeding on prickly pear. I could sense packrats, hiding from my noisy approach. Lizards and snakes, quail and doves, all hidden and sleeping.

I saw some deer, but they weren't like me. They were taller, with bigger ears. Their stag looked at me with interest, but I picked up my speed and soon left them all behind.

There was only one other like me and I was getting closer to her. I could feel her presence. I could feel her attention, drawn to me by the same thread of kinship that drew me to her.

And then suddenly there she was, descending from a ridge into a dry wash. She was so beautiful, her red fur glowing in the moonlight, her eyes deep as spring-fed pools.

I stopped a few paces from her, then we both moved forward at the same time, nuzzling each others' necks, her breath hot on my fur, mine on hers.

"<We should run, we should run,>" I said.

The sounds still came out as bleats, but they were bleats she could understand.

"<We should run,>" she agreed.

"<We will be together forever.>"

"<Forever,>" she repeated.

But before we could go, before we could run off into the night and let the moonlit desert swallow us, something dropped out of the sky, screeching, it's wings a storm of feathers in our faces.

We both jumped back, but only I understood what it was. A red-tailed hawk — that my sister could see as plainly as I did. But his sudden appearance brought a part of me up out of the soft warmth that was the deer to remind me that he was also a man.

A hawk man.

His name was...Anselmo...

He was sent...he was here to...I was supposed to remember...

As his wings bore him back up into the sky, I spilled out of my deer shape onto the ground. I was naked and shivering, goosebumps lifting from my skin. Worse, the connection — that wonderful, familiar connection we'd always had — was gone again. No, not gone entirely. But reduced to a thin trickle of energy.

The other deer shifted uneasily, ready to bolt.

No, I corrected myself. She wasn't a deer. She was...Laurel. Her name was Laurel. Just as my name was Bess. She was my sister. We weren't really deer at all.

Except...except...

The deer blood pulsed hard under my human skin, in my temples.

Laurel moved again, backing away from me now.

"No," I said.

I pitched my voice soft and didn't move except to hold my arms out to her.

"Please, Laurel. Don't go. It's me. Bess. I'm here to save you."

From what? a voice in me asked and I wasn't sure if the voice was mine or if it belonged to the deer in me. What did she need to be saved from?

But the deer that was Laurel stood still — held by the whisper of my voice, perhaps, or by the thin thread of sisterhood that still connected us, even though she was in animal shape and I wasn't.

"No," I said. "I guess you don't need to be saved. But don't...don't leave me behind, Laurel. Don't just go away and leave me."

Her large brown eyes regarded me and she made a querulous sound, low in her throat.

I didn't know what she was saying. But I didn't want to chance shifting back into a deer myself, either, just to find out. No, that's not true. I did want to shift back. I wanted it too much.

"Laurel," I said instead.

Shivering in the cool air, with my arms wrapped around me but doing nothing to keep me warm, I looked directly into her eyes and repeated her name. The third time I said it, she suddenly quivered. I saw something move in her eyes, and then all of a sudden, she was there, my Laurel, crouching naked on the ground.

She blinked, then grinned at me. Standing up, she ran her hands up from her shoulders and down her body, and suddenly she was wearing jeans and a cozy, hooded jersey, sneakers on her feet.

"How...how did you do that?" I asked.

She laughed. "Pretty cool, huh? Corina showed me. I can teach you how to do it, too, but first..." She stepped over to me. "Think of what you'd like to be wearing."

I don't know why, but all that came to mind was Frenchy from back home, in his long red underwear and overalls. And the next thing I know, that's what I'm wearing.

Laurel wrinkled her nose at my choice, but didn't stop smiling. Smiling? It was more than that. It was like every part of her was bursting with happiness. Her eyes were alive with good humor and she seemed to glow.

She also had the nubs of two little antlers growing from her brow.

"You...you've got horns," I said. "Or I guess I mean antlers. The start of them, anyway."

She stepped close. "So do you."

She reached out and touched my temple, then ran her hand up to the little antler bumps on my brow.

"They're so pretty," she said. "And furry."

I reached up to touch them. They did feel...pleasant. But of course, I'm always the worrywart.

"Do you think they're...permanent?" I asked.

Laurel shrugged, like she didn't care.

Another thing occurred to me. "I thought hinds — that's what we were, right? Female deer. I didn't think they even had antlers."

"They don't," a voice said from nearby.

We looked along the ridge to see Corina and Alice standing there in the moonlight with a large red dog by their side. Corina was the one who'd spoken.

As they moved closer, I saw that Alice still had those little antlers on her brow, but they were bigger than ours with three or four tines each. And then there were those long droopy rabbit ears of hers. She looked so cute, I thought, and wondered where all my fear of animal people had gone. Maybe once you'd been one, you couldn't be afraid anymore. I wasn't even afraid of being a deer again. To tell the truth, I sort of wanted it.

"When we come to the otherworld," Corina went on, "we tend to wear the shape most comfortable to us."

Was that why Jim was a red dog right now? Because he was more comfortable that way? Or was it his way of avoiding me? With him as a dog, we couldn't actually talk to each other.

"So they'll go away when we get back?" I asked.

Corina nodded. "They can go away right now if you will them to."

Oddly enough, all things considered, I didn't want to do that.

Laurel put her arm around my waist.

"It's not so bad, is it?" she said.

"No," I had to agree. "Just...strange. It takes some getting used to."

I looked up into the sky, but Anselmo was gone.

"He said to remind you about the Easter Ceremony," Alice said, knowing why I was looking.

"Who's 'he'?" Laurel asked.

"This hawk guy," I said. "The one that dropped from the sky just when we were thinking of running off..."

"Into forever," Laurel finished for me, her voice dreamy.

"Laurel, you won't — "

She gave me a squeeze. "Don't worry. I promise that if I go anywhere, I'll tell you first. Really, this time."

"Because it's scary," I said. "Not the part about being a deer, exactly. That was nice. But the feeling that nothing but being a deer mattered."

"It goes away as the deer shape becomes more familiar," Corina assured me. "You'll learn how to balance the two."

I nodded, not entirely sure.

"So what happens now?" I asked.

Alice laughed. "We should go back."

I gave a slow nod. "Of course."

But I hadn't been thinking about now. I'd been thinking about the whole rest of our lives. I had a million questions, but I guess I'd have to figure them out a day at a time, just like everyone else did with the puzzles in their own lives.

So we started back to where Corina had left her motorcycle because that was the closest to where the Hotel Congress was in our own world. Laurel walked ahead of me, with Corina and Alice on either side of her. The red dog fell in beside me. I almost patted him.

"Could you be less doggy?" I asked.

His shift was so fast it seemed like magic. Then I had to laugh. Of course it was magic. Everything here was magic.

"I'm sorry," he said. "About everything."

"Yeah," I told him. "Me, too. Maybe I overreacted a little."

He didn't say anything, but when I shot a look in his direction, I could see a hint of a smile playing on his lips. I looked away before I lost myself in those eyes of his.

I cleared my throat. "But you should have said something earlier."

"You're right. I should have. I was just being selfish. I wanted to steal those few days with you before you hated me."

I turned to him. "How could you know I'd hate you?"

"Do you?"

"I don't know. You made me mad. And scared me." I took a breath. "But how did you know I'd take it as badly as I did?"

He nodded to where the others walked ahead. "You're not like Laurel. The first time I saw her I could feel the yearning in her for something more. It's probably what first drew Corina to her as well."

"Maybe you should have picked her."

"I didn't *pick* anybody. There was no choice involved. As soon as I saw you, I knew I needed you. I still need you."

"But this whole business with Corina and the curse...I thought it was over."

"It is. My loving you hasn't got anything to do with that."

"Oh."

I remembered now that he'd said something about that earlier. I just hadn't wanted to hear it.

We walked along behind the others for awhile, not talking. The moon was on the horizon and it was darker now, but I didn't seem to have any trouble seeing through the shadows anymore. That was weird. Right. Like everything else wasn't.

"Us being different species...is that a problem?" I asked after awhile.

"We're not different species when we're in human form."

"Oh, right."

I was finding it so hard to stay mad at him. When I looked at everything from his point of view, mostly what had happened was me freaking out on him because of the circumstances of his birth, not because of who he was. And when you thought about it, there were a lot of things I hadn't told him either.

"So are you the kind of dog that chases after deer?" I asked.

He laughed. "Only one. And only if she wants me to."

Alice

Thomas met them in the doorway after Jim pulled his pickup in beside the Forester and the two of them approached the house.

"I'm beat," Jim said as soon as they came in through the door.

He gave Thomas a friendly nod, then went down to the guest room and closed the door behind him.

Alice watched him go, wondering how he was doing. He hadn't wanted to speak on the drive back from the hotel, so she hadn't pressed him, though she'd been dying to. Sometimes he was so hard to figure out.

She'd been surprised that he hadn't wanted to be with Bess. The two of them had seemed to be getting along, talking rather than arguing as they trailed along behind the others on the way back to where Corina had left her motorcycle. They'd even kissed before Bess had gone into the hotel with her sister, but it had been a chaste kiss — like that between friends — which left Alice only with the knowledge that they weren't enemies anymore. But was that it? Had all that fire between them simply died out, just like that?

"The girls are okay?" Thomas asked.

Alice turned back to him and nodded. "One of them got lost in the otherworld, so we had to go find her."

"And they're...safe?"

What he really meant was, were they unchanged?, Alice realized, so that was the question she answered.

"Yes. They're red deer women now."

His eyes clouded. "And they're okay with that?"

"Better than okay."

She smiled and took his hand, leading him into the living room.

"I know what you're going to say," he told her as they sat together on the sofa.

"No, you don't. I'm not going to ask you if you've changed your mind."

"Then what?"

She shrugged, then snuggled closer to him, leaning her head against his shoulder.

"I was going to say that this weekend's Easter."

"And you want to go to the pueblo."

She nodded. "But this time I want to watch the ceremony from the other side."

She could feel his disappointment.

"You want to go by yourself," he said.

"No. I want to go with you."

"But..."

"I know. That means I want you to come into *el entre* with me." She sat up and turned so that she could look at him. "It's funny, we've been arguing this back and forth for a long time, but something Jim said to me earlier today showed me how we'd been going about this all wrong. I keep trying to explain how it will benefit you and you — rightly — explain how those benefits aren't important to you."

"So what's different this time?" Thomas asked.

"This time I'm asking you to do it for me."

"Even when you know how uncomfortable it makes me?"

She nodded. "Because I don't want to lose you, Thomas. If you spend some time in the otherworld, we'll have that many more years together. Call me selfish or greedy or whatever you want, but I don't want to be alone. I want to be with you for as long as I can be. So, yes, I'm pushing you to do something that makes you uncomfortable, that you don't really want to do. But it's no different from you asking me to quit smoking all those years ago — remember?"

He gave a slow nod. "I asked you to do it for me."

"Even though it benefited me."

"I see."

He fell silent and they watched the sun rise above the Rincons through the east-facing window — as magical a light show as any sunset. Birds gathered at the feeder. The mourning doves stirred and began to coo from the brush. Quail ventured out into the sun.

"We haven't watched a sunrise together in a long time," Thomas said.

Alice nodded.

"I guess...I guess I'd like to see as many of them with you as I can."

Alice smiled and snuggled closer to him. Thomas put his arm around her.

"I'm sleepy," she said.

Thomas laughed. "I'll just bet you are."

He got up and pulled her to her feet and led her down the hall to their bedroom.

"You go ahead," she told him as they passed the bathroom. "I just have to pee."

When she was done, she went back into the hall. She paused by the door to the guest room, then cracked it open and peered in. The bed was empty and the window was open. She stood there for a moment, breathing in the creosote that drifted in on the breeze, before closing the door again and going on to her own bed where Thomas was waiting for her.

She pictured a red dog running out among the cacti and scrub, the sunlight waking highlights on his chestnut pelt.

Maybe he was running off his sadness, seeking the temporary oblivion that physical activity can offer.

She hoped he was running to his red deer woman, and that when he tapped on the door of her heart, she'd open it wide and let him in.

Laurel

"I can't believe you just let him go off like that," I said to Bess as we stood just inside the lobby and watched the taillights of Jim's pickup disappear around the corner.

"Everything was weird," she said. "So I told him I thought we should start over again, fresh."

She turned away and walked across the lobby, heading for the stairs. I followed along behind her. Our friendly desk clerk with all the piercings wasn't on duty. Sitting on his stool was a small woman with wonderfully fluorescent pink hair who gave us a nod and a smile before returning to the magazine she was reading. She didn't take any notice of what we were wearing, which, considering those red long johns that Bess had on, showed what I thought was admirable restraint.

"Start over how?" I asked.

"I told him he could try wooing me."

I had to smile. "You didn't actually use that word, did you?"

Bess ignored me. "I didn't want to seem easy. Adie always says to make the guy work a little."

"Yes, and our dear older sister has such a wonderful active love life."

"She did," Bess said. "And now she's got Lily."

I smiled, missing our little niece.

"I stand corrected. But 'wooing'?"

She looked over her shoulder at me and eloquently stuck out her tongue.

When we got back to our room, I flopped on the bed. I was so tired I thought I'd pass out, but my head was too abuzz with the night's adventures to allow me to sleep. Bess, of course, wasn't tired, having spent the whole of yesterday sleeping on the drive down and then here in our room.

"Show me how you did the thing with the clothes," she said.

So I did, and then lay on the bed watching her trying on outfit after outfit.

"You know you're being very girly," I said, "which isn't like you."

"I'm just practicing, that's all."

At the moment she was standing there in a lace teddy and panties that looked like they'd come right out of a Victoria's Secret catalog and that was *really* not her.

"Practicing what?" I asked. "Your own wooing techniques?"

"Get your mind out of the gutter."

"Hey, I'm not the one dolled up like a strollop."

"You think?"

I had to laugh. "I think you need somebody else's opinion — except you let him drive off into the sunrise."

She changed into a flannel shirt that hung low enough to be a nightie and sat on the bed with me.

"Do you think I blew it?"

I shook my head. "Not from the puppy dog eyes he was giving you when he left."

"Right. Thanks for bringing that up."

"It's just an expression."

"I know, but..."

She let her voice trail off and collapsed on the bed to lie beside me.

"How're you dealing with all of this?" I asked after a few moments.

"Better than I ever thought I would have." She turned her face to look at me. "I can't believe I'm saying this after the way I went on yesterday, but it's kind of cool."

"Kind of," I agreed.

"No," she said. "Way cool."

"All of it?"

"What do you mean?"

I held my hand up in the air and counted off. "Being a deer woman?"

"Running through the desert last night was amazing — plus I love this business with never having to think about buying clothes again."

"Your potential boyfriend is also a dog?"

"That's weirder, but...yeah. So long as he stays a guy when he's with me."

"Even when you're a deer?"

"I guess there are things we'd have to work out."

"And what about Alice?"

She sighed. "You were right about her, too."

I laid my hand on my stomach and shook my head.

"Wow," I said.

"I guess I was an idiot."

"No, you had good reason to be freaked. I mean, the last time..."

She shivered beside me and I knew that — just like me — she was thinking of when we'd been trapped underground by the 'sangmen, and then had to face down the whole host of the bee fairies, just the two of us with Sarah Jane.

"But this is different," she said, "and it got weird because it took me that much longer than you to figure it out."

"Well, I always was the smart one."

That earned me a poke in the ribs from her elbow, but I was very noble and didn't retaliate.

"I really want to go to the Yaqui Easter Ceremony," I said after awhile.

"On Saturday?"

I shook my head. "Alice said we should go after the gig on Friday night."

"Won't everything be over by then?"

"It goes all night. Some of the people will have been dancing for a whole week by the time Friday rolls around. We'll go Friday to see the forces of evil take over and then on Saturday the forces of good will prevail, keeping the world safe for another year."

"It sounds cool."

"I know. And then for Sunday, Alice is organizing some kind of musical jam back in the mountains in some canyon so that we'll get to meet and play with some of the local musicians."

"Human or cousin?"

I smiled at how easily the question rolled off her lips.

"Both."

"I wonder what kind of music —" Bess began, but she broke off.

We both sat up and looked at the window from where the sound had come. Howling.

Bess gave me a confused look. "What — ?"

I laughed. "I think someone's come wooing," I told her.

We both got up and went to the window, and sure enough, there in the parking lot was a dog, his fur the same chestnut red as Jim's hair. When he saw us at the window, he tilted his head back and howled again.

"What should I do?" Bess said.

"Well, I'm not giving up the bed," I told her.

She waved to him through the window, then stood in front of the mirror and started trying on clothes, her hands a blur as she went from one outfit to another.

"Don't forget that little lacy getup for underneath," I said.

She stuck out her tongue again, but this time I threw a pillow at her. Eventually she settled on the T-shirt and jeans she always wore.

"Oh, god, this is too weird," she said. "What am I going to say to him?"

I shook my head and steered her towards the door. "Who says you have to say anything? You're starting over again, aren't you? Just go have some fun."

She hesitated a moment longer, then she was out the door.

I went back to the window and watched her emerge onto the parking lot and approach the dog. It did what any dog would do and jumped up at her. I wasn't sure how she'd take it, but then I saw her laughing. The two of them headed off across Toole Avenue. I watched them until they disappeared behind the art studios beside the overflow parking lot, then I returned to the bed and lay down again.

I don't know if Bess realized it, but I knew why Jim had come the way he had. If she hadn't been able to accept the red dog, then there would have been no hope that they'd ever be able to work anything out. But as it was...

I smiled and closed my eyes.

So here I was, alone in a hotel room again, but I was too happy for them to be jealous. Besides, I still had Alejandro's business card in my purse. Who knows? I might give him a call after I finally got some sleep.

Corina

High above Gates Pass Boulevard, Corina sat down on a rock and looked away over Avra Valley. Though she still wore her turquoise jewelry, she fit in with the tourists today wearing cargo pants and a white T-shirt, a water bottle in hand.

Something stirred higher on the slope and she sighed when she spotted the rattlesnake making its way down to where she was. The snake became Ramona, fully-clothed and looking more human than Corina could ever remember her being.

"I'm not in the mood," Corina said before Ramona could speak. "So do us both a favor and save it for another day."

But Ramona surprised her.

"I owe you an apology," she said.

Corina could only look at her.

"I could have messed everything up," Ramona went on.

And that would matter to you because? Corina thought. But all she said was, "It all worked out in the end."

"No thanks to me."

Corina sighed then looked away, across the valley. "Not much thanks to me, either."

"I don't understand."

"All this meddling I do in people's lives — I think it ends up complicating things more than helping. Yes, it all worked out last night, but it was more touch-and-go than I'd care to repeat any time soon. I almost lost those girls."

"But you didn't."

Corina shrugged. "Like I said, no thanks to me. And for every half-assed success like that, I also have to deal with what happened with you and that bighorn man of yours."

"That wasn't your fault. Billy had every right to learn about his cousin blood. And besides, you were right. I would've gotten tired of him sooner or later."

Corina looked away from the view to study Ramona for a long moment.

"Why the sudden change of heart?" she asked.

"I met Rosa — in Prescott."

"Ah. And how is she these days?"

"You know her — I mean, personally?"

"I'm old, Ramona. Cody and I were already wandering these lands when she was still newborn."

Ramona nodded. "Sometimes I forget..."

"Sometimes I'd like to."

Neither of them spoke for a time.

"She was pretty amazing," Ramona said after awhile. "Her spirit's so...big."

"And what you see is what you get. No games, no pretension."

"She seemed to think I should be working on enlarging my own spirit."

"Good advice."

"So I was wondering...will you help me?"

Corina laughed. "Very funny."

"I'm serious."

Corina studied her again, longer this time.

"Damn," she finally said. "You are serious."

"So will you?"

"Even when I'm more likely to screw everything up? That old coyote curse I seem to be carrying just never gives up. Truth is, I'm surprised I'm not more of a pariah than I already am in certain circles."

"You should try carrying a snake's weight."

Corina smiled. "There's that."

"So," Ramona repeated. "Will you help me?"

Corina was quiet for a long time. The view of the valley pulled her gaze again — the vast wide space filling her heart. In the distance she could see the haze that was I'itoi's home, Baboquivari Peak, standing tall against the sky, the broken umbilical cord that once connected the sky to the earth.

When she turned back to Ramona, her eyes held a gleam of the mystery that lay at the spiraling heart of the mountain.

"Hell, why not?" she said. "I'll probably learn something myself."

Colorín colorado, este cuento se ha acabado.
The story has ended.